Ma

hadesgate

publications

Published by:
Hadesgate Publications
PO Box 167
Selby
YO8 4WP
Email: hadesgate@hotmail.co.uk
www.hadesgate.co.uk

Mage Reborn

Steve Dean

First published May 2007

Mailings to: Steve Dean
c/o Hadesgate Publications
PO Box 167
Selby
North Yorkshire
YO8 4WP
www.hadesgate.co.uk
www.hadesgateforums.co.uk

ISBN 978-0-9550314-7-2

Cover design by Ben Baldwin

Prepared and printed by:
York Publishing Services Ltd
64 Hallfield Road
Layerthorpe
York
YO31 7ZQ

Tel: 01904 431213   Website: www.yps-publishing.co.uk

Dedication

Dedicated with love and admiration to Julie Morledge, friend and sister (in deed if not in fact.)

Special Thanks to:

Garry Charles, of course.
Paula Charles, Ray Wilson and David Pearce at Hadesgate Publications, the World's number one publisher.

The Hadesgate Forum Crew for the hours of entertainment and laughing at my jokes.

And to all the agents and publishers who have sent me nice rejection letters over the years.

Part One

The Death of Magic

One

The axe blade bit deep into the woman's chest with a sound like splintering wood. The piercing scream that filled the high vaulted chamber didn't abate as her heart was pulled still beating from her living body. Only when the blood vessels were cut did the woman slump into lifeless silence. Her warm heart, dripping thick blood, was skewered onto the horn of the carved statue that stood behind a bone altar. Two other hearts already adorned the three- horned statue of OthmaDiarn, a man's and a child's, both equally fresh.

Setting aside the ceremonial axe, the priest removed a container from the carved mouth, into which the blood had collected. Carefully, he poured the blood into the saucer-like base of an ancient, but still shiny, candleholder, then placed it into position on the altar. A plain white candle was stood in the holder and lit. As the flame burned the blood began to creep up the candle, darkening its milky interior. When the blood reached high enough, the flame began to burn, a dark grey interwoven with threads of deepest red.

Thicker and faster the smoke rose, forming a solid shape above the flame. The priest threw wide his arms and opened his mouth, beckoning the presence of OthmaDiarn into his mortal soul, an act which would grant him immense power and life everlasting. Larger grew the cloud, now man sized, now as solid as flesh.

The candle flickered, as though a slight breeze had disturbed it. The priest's eyes widened, something was wrong. There wasn't a breath of air in this deep chamber. With mounting panic, the priest realised the cloud was out of control. The candle flame faded to yellow, the blood draining back into the holder, which was now tarnished and dull.

A scream to rival the screams of all three of the dead filled the chamber leaving no room for echoes. OthmaDiarn, his form no longer bound, had leapt into the priest's body. Three explosive blasts sounded in the underground room, each separate and distinct as the priest's body turned from whole to parts, to lumps, to pink mist.

Too late, OthmaDiarn realised he had destroyed the container of his essence in this world. Formless and drifting, he dissolved through the room, his inhuman death yell as unheard as the rest.

Less than a mile from the surface entrance to the vaulted chamber, a middle-aged man of indistinct features noted the tingling sensation cease in the hand that clutched a thick rod. He smiled, a pleasant, warm smile, then picked up his nap sack and moved on.

Two

The woman hissed through gritted teeth as the sharp knife dragged across her abdomen. She bit down on a thick leather strap to stop herself from crying out. Another sliding agony of pain locked her every muscle rigid as the knife moved again, this time deeper. The people around her held her tight as the pain threatened to black her out, but she fought against it, determined to stay conscious.

Another pain blossomed as probing hands reached inside her, took hold and pulled. Sighs of relieve sounded all around as the baby was tugged gently out of the womb and placed on her mother's chest by the birth healer.

No sooner had the mother looked down at the still wet baby than it was snatched from her. Voices whispered behind her, worriedly she cried out. Helpers held her tight as a healer stitched up the layers of her abdomen, but still the mother twisted her head for a sight of her baby. She relaxed as the infant was placed into the arms of a carved figure, a likeness of the Benevolent Mother. The eyes of the statue glinted with moisture as it looked down on the newborn child struggling for breath.

Those not involved with the mother gathered around as the child took first one breath, then another. A single wail, quickly cut off, silenced the room. One of the healers was pointing with a shaking finger at the face of the figure. The eyes of the statue had dried, a thin crack had appeared on the carved nose. As they watched in horror, it grew up and down the face, widening as it went. A healer with more presence of mind snatched up the baby as the crack travelled down the full length of the statue. Finally, the two halves parted, dropping to the stone floor with a dull thud.

All at once, the wailing began again, growing in volume until the whole town stopped to listen. In her mother's arms, the child drew breath, the first of many, and the last of the Benevolent Mother's children.

In the top room of a tavern only two streets away, a middle aged woman with long, dark hair, packed away a thick rod that had only just stopped humming. She added her velvet dress and the few pieces of jewellery she had worn to the bag, closed it and called for a servant. It was time to move on.

Three

Along a path that led straight to death, a figure stooped with the burden of age dragged himself wearily, one foot before the other. He was dressed in a plain hooded robe, which reached down to the everyday sandals he wore. His only other possession was a long staff on which he leaned, and which was remarkably heavy. Anyone who could have seen his eyes would have seen a power there, a power balanced almost perfectly by the energy contained in the staff. Almost.

He was dying, he knew that, being consumed from within by the battle with the magic, the only magic left in the world. It had been a long struggle, but he could smile, mostly because he wouldn't have to walk back.

Theirs had been a valiant battle, the Triangle of Nine, ridding the world of the evil of magic, but worth it in the end. Now man could live as it was always intended, could bloom again in a wholesome fashion.

Stopping to rest for a moment, the mage looked out across the landscape; rock, high hills, plains, but all yellowish rock. Nothing lived here, although many things died here. Not even the plants that thrived in other deserts could live in this place. Not a single animal or bird ventured into it or flew over it. Which was ideal for his purpose.

Setting off again, the mage died a little more as he crossed wills with the magic. It demanded to be free, but not here, not yet.

Later, he stopped again, looked around, trying to gauge whether he was far enough away from the nearest settlement. No, he decided, just a little further.

His will began to fail later in the day as the sun burned through his robe, parching his skin, drying his mouth. The mage stopped, this would have to be enough. There was still one thing left to do, and that would take the last of his will.

A smile cracked his lips. An irony, he thought, enough power to rend worlds gripped in his hand, yet he wasn't even allowed to create one last cool flask of water. Scanning all around one final time, seeing nothing but dust blowing on the hot breeze, he prepared himself.

The mage gathered his will, began summoning the last spell anyone would ever cast. With all his physical and mental strength he rammed the staff towards his knee, releasing the power that would keep him in one piece until the wood was broken. Energy surged through his body, cladding him in unbendable armour, giving him the might of giants. The staff impacted with his rising knee, cracking the wood in two, releasing a maelstrom of compressed magical energy in a single heartbeat. Strong though it was, the mages protective spell shattered like glass against granite, leaving him merely human in a storm of cosmic proportions.

The rock beneath the mage melted, a wave of energy flowed outwards, rippling the ground like waves on the sea. The centre flew upwards, miles into the hot air. A sound like giant drums boomed across the empty land, echoing around the hills and plains. From a safe distance, which was several hours walk, a blinding flash of many colours was seen, followed by a cloud, like a thick stalk topped by a spreading cap.

Only a few hours later, all that remained was a smooth sided crater and a strange rippled landscape three miles across.

Four

A spike was driven into his ankle, fastening him to the searing rock. Blood from three similar wounds had already joined with the redness leaking from his other injuries, as it ran down the sloping face of a large boulder. Lifeblood gathered in a crack by his feet, mixing with wind blown sand. The four soldiers backed off, admiring their work. It wasn't easy to hammer metal into this type of rock, it tended to crack and the spikes fell out. With a nod of satisfaction, the leader gathered up the emperor's men and led them away, each spitting on the captive for good measure.

The sun soon dried the blood on the rock, and raised blisters on the already tortured skin of the young man. Very close to death, the pain had long since faded into a narrowing blackness. With lips swollen and cracked, the man mumbled curses against the emperor mixed with cries for help. The sun rose and set, but he still clung to life, his body stubbornly refusing to release him. Finally, he didn't know how many days later, he reached the last seconds of his life, ticking by as the beats of his failing heart slowed. Beat. Beat.

Beat.

Beat...

The sky lit with a blinding light, a mighty boom echoed around his head and the rock he was fastened to dropped backwards into an avalanche of tumbling, vibrating stone. The captive gasped, assuming this was the end of his existence. He prepared as best he could to meet whomever the priests had said would be there. A deep chasm opened under him, dropping the rock and its passenger into its boiling depths, then closed over him.

Part Two

Rebirth

One

"And that was a thousand and a hundred years ago, according to the book of Sagix."

The young wizard sat at rapt attention, her grey eyes wide with awe, as the old wizard re-told the ancient stories. The old man continued. "But as we now know, the magic wasn't destroyed, just spread out again, as it had been in the beginning, but the olden mages weren't learned enough to see this, else too learned. Then a man named..?" The wizard pointed at K'treema.

"Iray Wisehand," she answered without hesitation.

The wizard smiled, "And what comes from that name?"

"The word 'wizard', wizard B'drato," she replied just as quickly.

"Good, K'treema, you pay attention. In a wizard that is a prime quality. You must pay attention to all things at all times."

The old man stretched out, easing a dull ache in tired legs. "The old ones had power, power we can only imagine. The stories tell of great magical battles, raging fire and lightning smashing down castle walls and destroying whole armies. These are some of the things lost to us, along with magic rings and wands, magic boats and flying things. But, if we all study hard enough, who knows, one day one of you may bring down castle walls, with just your tiny finger." B'drato crooked his age-blighted digit, smiling at his class of youngsters. They laughed.

"Off you go then, but remember, study everything, miss nothing."

K'treema bade farewell to her tutor and the classmates she knew well, and headed for home. On the way she tried to look at every single thing around her, counting the adobe houses as she passed them, listed the colours of the garments hanging to dry in the warm breeze, tried desperately to name all the animals as they wandered across her sight. It wasn't easy; sometimes she wished she hadn't been found at the annual wizard trials. But then she would light her lamp with just a thought, and then she was so glad she had.

Arriving home, she called out to her parents as they sat in the garden enjoying the evening sun. Their house was on a hill overlooking the wide green valley that provided much of the areas wealth. Cattle, horses and deer were raised on the lush grass that grew all year round. K'treema entered the house and climbed the steps to her room. Her window looked out upon the hill, but she didn't mind, who wanted to look at boring cows any way?

Just before she opened her door, she imagined her small lamp lit, glowing a soft orange by her bed. Then she held the image, picturing every detail. She filled in the rest of the colours, the flickering of the small flame, the shadows cast by the small doll and the books piled all around. On entering she cried out in triumph, the lamp was lit, illuminating the room just as she had seen it in her head. That had been the first time she had managed it through the door. Dropping her study books on the bed, she went over to the window and opened the shutters. But instead of looking out like most would, she looked up, past the few clouds and up to the sky that would soon bear stars.

Often she wondered what they were, she had heard many stories, some of them just plain silly, but she promised herself that one day she would find out.

With diligent study and much practise, K'treema soon became B'drato's best pupil, showing wisdom beyond her years and a caring for others the old man approved of. He decided it was time for her to see the world, to venture out on the journey all wizards completed in order to gain knowledge, without which she was only half trained. B'drato sent a message to a friend, asking him if he knew of a suitable travelling companion or two who could link up with her. Wizards never travelled alone, two was safer, but also introduced a second viewpoint, often of greater value than all the book learning a tutor could muster.

Soon, an excited K'treema, now a young woman, bid her family a tearful farewell, and set off to meet her companion at the port half a days journey north. B'drato went with her, to see all was well.

Two

A small figure huddled in the stern of a sea going vessel trying not to be sick. She was wet, cold and tired, sleep being impossible with this constant and unfamiliar motion. She hadn't really eaten either but she preferred not to think about that. For three days the ship had creaked and splashed its way along the coast, travelling so slowly, she thought at times they were going backwards.

Why couldn't she have gone by land? A day's journey over the mountains and she would have been there. But no, father said it was dangerous, it was much safer to go around, even if it took ten days. At this rate it would take even longer.

All for nothing too, all because some doddering old wrinkle-arse had said she had the wizards' power, when not once had she been able to do anything magic. For the hundredth time today she drew in a deep breath and let out a self-indulgent sigh. The helmsman, standing at the wheel a few paces away, ignored her, he'd heard it all before.

Shemaz supposed she ought to make the effort to walk over to the water barrel, she was very dry inside, but the thought of going down to the latrine filled her with dread. Only at night, when the wind calmed somewhat and the ship steadied a little, could she go below to wash and relieve herself.

Pulling the damp, salt encrusted blanket tighter around her neck, Shemaz looked up at the flapping sails. She was no expert, indeed had never even been on a boat before, but she was sure the sails should be filled with wind, pulled tight by its force. A fleeting thought whispered across her mind, perhaps she should tell the sailors. No, better not, they probably wouldn't appreciate it. After all, she was only a farmer's child, she knew nothing of the sea, had never even seen it until a few days ago, not this close anyway.

For two days and more she had bundled herself in this blanket, taken her seat on the hard deck, and still been green with sickness. Despite being blown with sea spray and suffering the mocking laughter of passing sailors, she was forced to endure, for here was the only place on the entire ship that she didn't actually vomit.

Pulling up the blanket until only her blue eyes and the top of her blonde head showed, she muttered to herself, cursing the wizard, her father, her teacher, and anyone else who had the slightest link to her journey. Especially the sailors, those grinning, monkey-faced, slimy, not at all seasick idiots, clambering around those silly ropes like hairy-legged spiders.

Why couldn't the sails fill with wind? She wailed under her breath. Just a few blasts and the ship would speed along. Surely that wasn't too much to ask?

Shemaz found that keeping her eyes on the sails made her feel worse, so she looked straight up, at the slow moving clouds high above. For a while this relaxed her, a wind blew across her forehead, cooling her heated brow. The clouds moved in a different direction to the ship, something she found odd. Surely the clouds were blown by the same wind?

Shemaz tried to study the wind, watching the clouds, then the wind fluttering the sails. It all seemed so chaotic, no order at all. Wouldn't it be better if the wind flowed smoothly? She stared at the clouds, and then moved her head, trying to keep the same focus as she looked at the sails. It was no good; she simply couldn't see the air moving, only the effect of it.

The sickness returning to her stomach was the only indication that it had momentarily gone. Whilst she studied the clouds she had forgotten completely about her condition. Quickly, she looked up again, and began to look from mast to sky, searching out the finer movement of the wind.

She tried to image what wind would look like, and decided that ribbons, themselves blown by a breeze, were the nearest thing she could think of.

And there they were.

She was so startled she sat upright with a gasp, assuming her lack of sleep and water had induced a fever. Almost shyly she looked again, pictured the ribbons.

A grey ribbon flowed from behind the ship and into the sail, a bulge appeared where it impacted, and then slowly drooped as the ribbon curled away from the sail and around the ship. Shemaz sat bolt upright. No, come back, she thought furiously, but the ribbon ripped to shreds as she tried to retrieve it.

Slumping back into her original position, she watched the ribbons; some grey, some white, some red, as they swam and entwined across the sky, lazily curling and criss-crossing in a casual fashion that infuriated Shemaz.

Finally, she could take it no longer. Seating herself as comfortably as possible, she calmed herself, and began to pull the ribbons into the sails. The old wizard had told her magic came from the pictures in your mind, one merely had to imagine something to be true for it to actually be true. One by one ribbons of wind flew into the sail, pressing and bulging the canvas. The sailors began to stop and look up as the ship slowed. Not at all the effect she was after, Shemaz stopped concentrating and let the ribbons have their freedom. A knot of ribbons writhed before the sails, then broke apart, allowing the ones behind to once again drive the ship. Shemaz slumped back, her sickness forgotten for the moment, but she was no closer to where she wanted to be.

A few minutes later, she noticed a large ribbon of wind approaching the ship from the left side, was that port or starboard? The ribbon angled towards the sails, then at the last second was knocked away by another. Shemaz was almost audibly seething with anger, so when another came by and was about to be knocked away, she grabbed the offending ribbon and stopped it, causing it to break up. The first ribbon was now free to hit the sails, which belled nicely against its force.

Looking around, Shemaz found that many of the ribbons that would otherwise miss could be made to hit the sails if given a little nudge. Others that approached at the wrong angle could be straightened, doubling their effectiveness.

For the first time in three days, Shemaz smiled, almost giggled, as the sails filled and the old ship, with a creaking of rope and a slapping of canvas, bit through the waves, surging forwards under the tamed wind.

Three days later, a full four days early, the ship arrived at the port of Sahgony. The captain was whisked away by other seafarers and ensconced in the local tavern where he was plied with drinks and entreated to tell his story. For most of the night, and the rest of his life, he would earn free drinks telling the tale of how he traversed the point of Calasha, a notorious spot of contrary winds, in only half a day.

A tired, thirsty, and ravenous Shemaz hopped onto the quay, a smile on her face. Well, she thought, that was exhilarating, must do it again some time.

Three

Beat...

Beat.

Beat. Beat. His heart didn't stop, but carried on, thumping in his chest as the magic energy washed through him. Fading life was snatched up and repaired, wounds were healed, the tortured body made whole. Still the magic seethed and burned, all around him a sparkle of power chased and flowed. He was nourished by it, and then improved, as the energy was thrust into every cell, into his mind and heart.

Years past, then more, until one millennium had gone and another started. Buried under the rocks of the place called Death, he lay undisturbed, whilst the magic faded and spread through the rocks. Then, one day, the wind and heat flaked off a final piece of rock and sunlight flashed into the buried chasm.

A point of light appeared, he tried to shield his eyes, but was somehow pinned down. Unable to do anything but close tight his eyes, he endured the light, like so many other things in his life.

A pulsing in his arms and legs grew, making him uncomfortable. Realising he was trapped under a massive rock fall, the man should have panicked, but found only calm in the depths of his mind. Cautiously, he tried to reach out with his hand, and found the rocks slid apart easily. He did the same with the rest of his limbs, and then stood, forcing hard stone aside like he was rising from a feather filled cover on a soft bed.

A few more swimming movements found the man atop the low hillside under which he had lain. The land around was warm, and had a pleasant yellow tinge to his eye. Nothing moved beside himself, this also he approved of. A thirst niggled at him, but he ignored it, there was time for that later. First he had something to do, but he couldn't remember what.

He sat on a small rock, picked up a stone and melted it to orange lava in his hand. With a few well-placed pinches, he made a small animal, possibly a dog or cat. Then he threw it into the air. Several seconds later it came back down, landing in his out stretched hand, although his eyes were shut tight.

Slowly, he opened his eyes and focused on the stone. Fragments of memory returned, a woman, blonde hair and smiling, a man, laughing into his face, pain, lots of pain. Then he remembered. He stood, turned all around, and then shouted. "My name is Dhomag, and I have vowed to kill the Emperor."

Four

The noise was deafening. Battle raged all around, metal against metal, against wood, against flesh. Death screams filled the air, shrieking, roars of triumph, bellowing. They were losing, being driven back by superior forces. Then the ground began to rumble, a ripple spread across the surface. Just before the line of enemy wizards, a gigantic head broke from the ground. Horns like sharpened tree trunks, eyes of fire, a mouth that gave forth a baking breath. The ground ignited as the gagrog burst from the soil.

The enemy wizards launched spell after spell against the fiery behemoth, all to no avail. Strangely, a woman sat atop the beast, lounging between the horns like a queen on a parade. Her long legs bare, her black hair streaming in the wind.

The wizards turned their attention to her, but their magic was repelled by the presence of the gagrog. The woman turned her head, searching, as if for a certain target. Eyes fell upon green eyes, locked. The gargantuan creature, sensing its mistress' wish, turned its bulk towards the target. A mouth wider than the city gates opened. Heat and stench from the breath would have melted stone. One thundering step after another, the beast moved, eating up the ground with its long strides. The green-eyed woman tried to scream, but her mouth was frozen closed, tried to run, but her legs wouldn't move. The gagrog stamped closer, and then lifted a taloned paw to crush her to pulp.

She sat upright, sweat dripping from her naked body, soaking the bed sheets. She took several deep breaths, steadying her heartbeat. When she was calm enough, the woman turned up the tiny glow of her bedside lantern, lighting the room with a soft yellow light. Padding over to the window, she threw back the shutters and stood in the cooling breeze. As the sweat evaporated and her racing heart quieted, a smile spread across her face. For this had been no nightmare, but a vision. The woman atop the beast, controlling its unstoppable rampage, was she herself, princess Oleana-tarli of the house of Iamun, soon to be queen Oleana-tarli.

The smile widened. The princess stepped out onto the moonlit terrace and slid into a reclined chair. Her hands moved over her soft skin, cupping and caressing her breasts, fingering her large nipples. With a sigh, she ran her left hand slowly down her stomach and over her pubic mound, slipping into the already damp slit. A deeper sigh escaped her mouth as she began to move her fingers back and forth, widening her legs until her feet touched the floor either side of the chair.

On the palace wall just above the terrace, in the shadows of a turret, a lone guard watched the princess and began to loosen his armour. His hand slipped inside and started to rub his hot erection in time to the princess' rhythm.

Oleana-tarli wondered how much the soldier had to give to get this posting each night, for she knew it was the same man, she could sense that. The princess could also sense the man's rising pleasure, adding to her own. Her fingers moved faster and faster, her moans louder and louder. They shared a climax that night, and never even met, the soldier completely unsuspecting that the princess was aware of his every emotion.

Five

Dhomag walked purposefully in a straight line, but not really knowing where he wanted to be. He had decided to head west, not actually knowing why, but intent none the less. The sun burned down, as it always did in the land called Death, but Dhomag felt only a balmy breeze and the pleasant warmth of a summer afternoon.

He saw no other life as he walked, though there appeared to be some, even in this place. A thirst played on his lips, but never grew to anything more. And a niggling hunger fluttered around his stomach; with nothing to eat he ignored it. By day he walked, one foot in front of the other, thinking nothing in particular. By night, when Death gave up its heat like an upturned pan gives up its water, he formed a Dhomag-shaped hollow in the rock and slept a dreamless sleep.

After a handful of days, he heard voices in the distance, just to one side of his route. He decided to ask whomever he found there for directions to the emperor's palace.

A wooden structure had been built against one wall of a narrow canyon. It was a simple shelter, a thatched roof held up by posts, providing shade from the ever-present sun.

Six men lay or sat around in a scooped out hollow below it. For a few moments he studied the men, who appeared to be soldiers of some kind. Their armour was deep red leather with a stylised bird of prey embossed in the chest plate. All the men had shoulder length hair of various colours, from medium to dark brown. They wore short swords and carried small oval shields with the same device painted on. Not far from where they lounged, each man had rested a crossbow, loaded and ready. Seven horses stood tied together at the furthest end of the canyon, chewing noisily on sacks attached to their halters.

Dhomag announced himself. "Good day, my name is Dhomag, could someone please tell me where I might find the emperor?"

The six men jumped up as he spoke and were on their feet, swords pointed at him before he could finish the sentence.

"How did you get so close without us seeing?" One of them asked.

"And what do you want with the emperor?" Another asked, moving closer and jabbing the point of his sword towards Dhomag.

Dhomag decided to ignore the first question and answer the second, as it seemed more related to his quest. "I am going to kill him."

The soldiers laughed. "What with, your bad breath?" They roared, echoing laughter off the rock walls.

"No, I'm going to nail him to a rock."

They laughed again. Three of the men approached Dhomag until they were almost touching, he could smell the stale sweat pulsing off their over heated bodies. "First, you are going in completely the wrong direction, in that the emperor lives east of here. Second, you haven't got nails nor a hammer with which to do it. Third, I think the sun has got to you, if you think the emperor is going to let you just walk over to him nice as day and stand still whilst you nail him to a rock."

"Who is he and where is he going? Looks to me like a spy, so we're going to have to kill him, this one," another added.

The third glared at him, as if he could stare a confession out of him. Dhomag looked at the men, one by one, saw no threat, and turned to walk away. A shout went up, a hand grabbed his shoulder and spun him around. A hot rush of power flared within him at the soldier's touch. As the point of the sword neared his stomach, a wall of energy sprung to life, causing the sword to stop, as though impacting against iron.

The soldier looked down, his mouth falling open.

"He's got armour on under those rags, he is a spy." Came a shout.

The soldier stepped back and swung his sword, both hands on the grip. Before the arc could complete, Dhomag punched the man, knocking him several strides back and cracking neck and jaw. The man was still airborne when he died.

The twang of two or three crossbows sounded in the hollow, sending deadly steel tipped shafts flying towards him. Just missing their comrades, who yelled out as the missiles buzzed past, the bolts burst into flames a few inches from Dhomag's skin, then dropped to the floor and broke into pieces of charcoal.

Two of the soldiers rushed him, one from each side, as those behind re-loaded their crossbows. Dhomag pointed a finger at each of the men. A ball of light no bigger than a fingertip shot from each outstretched hand. Less than a blink later, both men slumped to the ground, a neat, bloodless hole burned right through their heads. The men loading their crossbows stopped, looked at their fallen comrades, and slowly lowered their weapons to the rocky floor, stepping away from them. Smiling nervously, one of them spoke in a quavering voice. "We aren't going to hurt you, it was their idea it was, see, we put our crossbows down we did. No trouble, you want the emperor, just head east, when you get to a town, they'll tell you from there. It's not far."

Dhomag turned his head and looked back the way he had come. No choice then but to head east. He turned and began to walk away. Just as the soldiers began to think he was going, Dhomag whipped round and launched several balls of light towards them, shooting them with a slight whooshing sound. The soldiers dropped to the floor with a clank of swords and daggers. Dhomag walked back and examined his handiwork. Each man had three holes burned through him, one in the head and two in the chest, and not a drop of blood. He was going to enjoy killing the emperor, but first he had all those soldiers to practice on.

A short distance away, cowered behind a rock, his leather trousers still around his ankles, the seventh soldier squatted above a steaming pile of dung. His mouth hung open, his mind stuck on a single thought. A word trembled on his lips but wouldn't come out. "Mu,mu,mu," he mumbled. Inside his head the word screamed loudly.

"Mage!"

Six

Along a lonely road that followed the sea, a pair of travellers stopped suddenly at the sound of horses. Looking quickly around with nervous eyes, the two searched for a hiding place, but none was apparent in the flat landscape, except for a grove of fruit trees too far away to be of use. Up ahead, the road disappeared into a small copse of shivangh trees, their yellow blossoms rippling on the slight breeze. It was from there that the sounds came; metal clicking and the steady thud of hoofs.

K'treema moved to the side of the road, gesturing for Shemaz to follow. They continued walking, heads up, alert but trying not to be threatening. After all, two young, modestly dressed people travelling together could only be wizards. And wizards weren't to be interfered with. K'treema repeated this to herself as they walked. Inside, a warm feeling began to grow, and in her head she began to imagine a large fist, battering into a tall stranger.

Of course they had been told the road was safe. It was patrolled regularly by the Emperor's own men, guarding the coast against marauders, pirates and other wrong doers, jealous of the empires' wealth and prosperity.

She could hear Shemaz walking slowly behind her, took comfort from her presence. Even though they had only known each other a short time they had got on famously, almost from the start. They had even chosen similar gifts to give each other from the harbour market. It was traditional to exchange small tokens with your travelling companions, it was seen as the first bond, in that each owned something of the others. The two wizards had been very surprised when they had both presented each other with a coral necklace. K'treema's gift from Shemaz was a line of fish each carved from a single piece of red coral, Shemaz's was a sea serpent, made up of different coloured pieces. Both were threaded onto strong leather and fastened with a metal clasp.

It had been a pleasant journey so far, if a little dull, but K'treema was wise enough to know this was better than too much excitement.

The taller wizard glanced over her shoulder, making eye contact with Shemaz, who smiled back reassuringly. Shemaz, though younger and shorter by a full hand width, seemed to have greater confidence, but was a little vague about her wizard power. B'drato had told her that sometimes wizards took a while to develop their power, even into adulthood. K'treema suspected that Shemaz hadn't yet got full control of hers.

Smiling to herself, K'treema remembered their first camp, when she had startled Mazzy by lighting the fire with her power. Shemaz had scuttled backwards as the small pile of sticks became instantly alight.

The first horse emerged from the copse, leather barding dull in the shadows. More emerged, all alike, complete with leather-armoured men, neat and uniform. Only the second rider on the left showed any variation, as he held a fluttering banner on a short lance. The triangular red pennant bore the symbol of a large black cat, thickly manned and long in the body.

K'treema smiled, these were the emperor's men, the legendary coastal defence lancers, fast, strong and deadly. Some said they were the best horsemen in the land, others that they were deadlier when un-horsed, with their twin short swords and short bows.

As the column drew level, the lead horse stopped, the rest coming to a complete halt almost instantly, and not a single signal had passed between them. The captain turned his liquid grey eyes on the two wizards, who almost melted at the sight. He was the most handsome man K'treema had ever seen. A strange feeling tickled her heart, moved through her stomach and settled very disconcertingly between her legs.

"Good day to you wise ones, you are well I hope?" the captain asked, removing his tri-cornered hat and sweeping it wide as he bowed stiffly from the saddle.

"Yes thank you, sir," K'treema answered. Shemaz smiled, very sweetly K'treema thought, but said nothing.

"Off on your travels then? Where are you headed? Ah! what it's like to be young again." The soldier leaned down, and whispered, "I wish I was going with you."

Shemaz spoke up now, "Well sir, you may join us any time. We are off to Ga Vul, along the coast, then probably inland to see the fair city of Esh, from there we haven't yet decided."

"We'll probably end up in Oq, everyone says we will, drawn there as all who travel are." K'treema added.

"Oh, yes. Our mighty capital and home of the Emperor himself, no doubt you will have the times of your life there, but be careful, there are many who are only too willing to earn a dishonest living from pretty young ladies like yourselves." The captain preened his hair and waited whilst his compliment was absorbed. "But tell me wise one, you are not from Sahgony, I would guess by the slight difference in your speech that you are from beyond the mountains, where it is said all girls are pretty and all men very happy. Alas I have never been, to my hearts shame."

"Yes sir, I am from Deetra's pass, a small town that overlooks the coastal plain. How clever of you to notice." Shemaz smiled as warmly as she could manage.

The soldier waved his hand, as if batting away the compliment. "You are too kind to an old soldier, wise one. But alas I must be going, we have a coastline to patrol if you are to sleep unmolested tonight. Travel well, the coast we have just patrolled is safe, you have my word." Clutching one hand to his chest, he slapped his hat back on and moved his horse forwards. Instantly, the whole column was on the move, clumping along the sandy road.

The two companions looked at each other and sighed. Giggling, they stepped back onto the road and moved on, pushing and teasing each other, getting lewder and louder about various parts of a man's anatomy. After a while it became obvious that both were guessing when it came to the kind of things men and women did together. Shemaz had seen goats climbing on each other's backs, the male pushing his long pink prod towards the female. K'treema agreed that it was probably much the same with people.

She had seen a naked man herself, although she refused to say who or where and went very red when Shemaz repeatedly asked.

"What I don't understand," K'treema said, "is how the goats thing can stick out. The man I saw had a droopy one, and it was very small." She flushed a deep scarlet as Shemaz laughed.

"Sorry 'Tree, I wasn't laughing at you. It was just the disappointment on your face when you said it."

They both laughed aloud, a shrieking giggle that startled a flock of dark birds out of a low clump of grass.

By now they had reached the copse, and so both fell silent. Studying the shadows cast by the multi-trunked trees, they walked briskly until they emerged safely on the other side. Both immediately began to laugh again, alternately clamping hands over their mouths, or desperately shushing each other.

Seven

Princess Oleana-tarli was naked, as usual, when the guard she had summoned arrived. The woman, dressed in the usual red leather of the king's soldiers, stood firmly to attention by the door. Of late, well, since she had become a woman really, her male guards had slowly disappeared, and been replaced by women. When she had asked her father, he had said the men were needed elsewhere, and only women were available. But she did manage to get a promise out of him, to return the men as soon as they were free. But that didn't stop this guard looking at her in that way her male guards used to.

Smiling, she beckoned the guard over. "It seems I am to be taken into the presence of the king. I can't go like this now can I?"

The guard hesitated just a fraction before she answered. "No, your highness."

"Then you must dress me."

"But highness, do you not have serving ladies?" The guard queried, her deep brown eyes widening with barely controlled joy.

"They have all left me, busy on some silly errand. You will have to do it." The princes smiled slyly.

"Yes your highness, of course." The guard breathed deeply, her broad chest barely restrained by the toggles on the sides of her armour.

Princess Oleana-tarli spread her legs slightly and raised her arms. "Let's start with the under clothes then, it's those soft, silky, pink ones over there."

"Yes highness." The guard breathed, fetching the indicated apparel. The cloth was barely felt on her rough hands, but it sent a thrill of feeling up her backbone.

"Kneel down, I have to step into those."

The guard knelt. As she lowered the clothes to the royal ankle, a spicy scent wafted over her nostrils, arousing her like no man ever could. The princess had bowed forward, pushing her pubic mound right next to the guard's face.

With supreme effort, the guard managed to stand upright and pull the underwear around the Princess's waist. Such a pity to cover a beautiful sight, she thought, but now her hands were next to the Princess's full breasts. Her eyes locked on to the gently bobbing nipples as Oleana-tarli breathed slowly, watching the guard's every expression.

A scream shrilled around the palace, out of the open window, along the corridors of the princess's chamber. Guards and servants and aides appeared from every direction, the minor chores they had been sent on forgotten.

"She touched me, she touched the royal person," shrieked the princess indignantly, clutching a long gown to hide her semi naked person. The king's Chamberlain of Gowns arrived, evaluated the scene with a flick of her gimlet eyes and immediately took charge.

"Guards, seize that retched perpetrator and have her

flogged, ten lashes, then set her to guard the entrance to the royal privy." The chamberlain knew the princess well, normally anyone touching the royal person without leave would die on the spot, but guards were hard to replace, and the princess had gone through several until the king caught on to her games.

"You, all but the princess' lady, out." She waited whilst the room was cleared of none armour wearing staff, apart from a small fair skinned woman who was comforting the princess, from a discrete distance.

"Now, your highness, excitement over, the king is waiting."

Meekly, the princess allowed herself to be dressed, then followed the chamberlain, actually a lady of great wisdom and power herself, along the corridors to the king's audience chamber.

The king, a tall, thin man, with bushy blond hair and a permanent smile, was sat on his over stuffed throne reading a long parchment. Always, no matter where or when anyone entered the king's presence, he was reading a long parchment or a thick book. And never, no matter how many times you entered his presence, was he ever seen to finish one.

"My dear, come, sit by me, we have a little business to attend to. One day you will be queen, so no matter how boring it may seem, you must learn to receive visitors." Seeing the princess' bored look, and interpreting it as worry, he continued. "Now dear, don't worry, I have started you off on an easy one. A soldier, who wishes to speak with his Highest on a matter of some importance. I have had my aides talk with him but he is insistent the news is of such shattering consequence only my ear will do. I tell you, if this is about how poor he is and how many children he's got to feed, I'll cut his nuts off and tell him to go boil them up for supper. That'll feed his children and stop him getting any more." The king looked around the room, one by one his aides roared with laughter.

The princess sat on the lower seat next to the throne, and settled herself for a long, boring afternoon.

With little ceremony, the doors at the opposite end of the chamber opened, revealing a small figure book-ended by two enormous guards. Her eyes were immediately drawn to the red leather clad men. There was something about leather, and particularly red leather, that made her warm inside. It was probably something she got off her father, as it was the king who ordered the change from dull brown to full blooded scarlet.

As the guards approached she heard the creaking of armour all around as the soldiers behind the throne tensed, ready for any attack on the king. It wasn't really fair, she thought, all these male guards and not one to spare for her.

The small figure wasn't as small as he had seemed when framed by the guards and the high doorway. In fact it was the guards who were tall, the man being more average in height. He was in his late twenties, had black hair and a circular scar on his left cheek. His face bore one or two bruises where the king's aides had talked with him, and his lips were cracked as though he hadn't drunk for a while. He was pushed to his knees in front of the throne.

"You may speak man, and make it quick, I warn you it had better be good, or your children will eat well tonight." The chamber filled with laughter, but the man's face creased with puzzlement. Nevertheless, he swallowed deeply, took a breath and spoke, his voice strong and sure. "Highest, I bring you news of great importance. My men are all dead, killed by a mage..."

Once again the throne room was filled with laughter. All but the princess, who was suddenly intensely interested, laughed scornfully at the man's words.

"No, Highest, I swear on my best horse's life, it is true. This man walked into the border post and melted holes through my men. They fought bravely, with sword and crossbow, but no weapon would touch him. Quarrels burst into flames as they neared. He pointed at them and they died. I swear every word is true Highest."

"This man, this so called mage, where did he come from? The books tell us the mages were destroyed by their own kind over a thousand years ago, are you saying this man was that old?"

"No, Highest, he was young, younger even than I. I don't know from where he came, he just arrived, said he was going to kill the emperor, and we all laughed."

The king sat upright, several military advisers almost spilled their wine. "He said he was going to kill the emperor? And you tried to kill him? Are you mad? You should have seen to it that he had all the help he could get. Now, tell me from the beginning what happened, and miss no detail."

The king settled back to listen as the man related his tale. The princess visibly tensed as the details emerged. This was a sign, if the mages had returned, that meant her vision was about to become reality. The gagrog awaited her; all she needed was to find out where.

When the man fell into silence, the king stood. "What is your name man?"

"Falco, Highest, Falco Tarm, corporal of ten in the King's Own Skirmishers, Your Highest." The man stood taller as he proudly stated his name and rank.

"Well, Falco Tarm, corporal of ten, you will go back and find this man, and see to it that he gets every opportunity to fulfil his quest. We are nothing if not generous in these matters. Go, and don't come back without good news."

Falco stood to attention. "Yes your Highest, and how many men will I take?.. Highest."

"Men corporal? You had some men, we gave you some and you lost them, we can't afford to keep giving them to you indefinitely. Now, off you go, and you'd better take plenty of water and a good, strong metal breast plate, just in case the 'mage' takes a dislike to you."

The aides roared with laughter, this time without prompting. The man turned and was escorted out of the king's presence.

The king himself smiled widely. "Did you hear that? Fortune indeed smiles on us. General, is all prepared for the invasion?"

A small man with a large belly snapped to attention. "Indeed Highest, there is enough water stashed in the desert to keep an army alive. Scout parties have been sent, and just this morning I received a messenger bird from one of them informing me that a water source had been found beyond the lands called Death, one that can be captured easily. My men are ready to go sire." The general dropped to one knee and lowered his head.

"Excellent, now send a message back. I want five hundred men across the desert in ten days..."

"Ten days Highest? But it takes fifteen days at least, there is a lot of it Highest, the men will have to fight on the other side too." The general interrupted, a sweat breaking out on his forehead.

"...time, where they will meet with the scout party and capture the water, and as many horses as they can find. The main force of the army will set out at the same time, at a slower rate. Send the cavalry afoot, we don't want to waste good horses when they can find some on the other side. They do still have horses in the empire I suppose, or have they come up with some new invention?"

"Yes, Highest, they still use them, what can ever replace a good steed Highest?"

"What indeed. But enough of this, you have your orders general, I want Esh captured before the day of the Feast of the Rich Waters. From there it's only a short massacre to Oq, and the emperor's death day." The king sat back, his eyes lost focus and a slight smile appeared on his lips. Those who knew him well knew what this meant. There would be no more sense out of him today.

* * * * *

Some time later, after sneaking away from her father, the princess was ensconced in the large royal library. She was fully clothed in modest robes, and was even wearing shoes. There was something about books that made her feel uncomfortable to be near when she was naked.

Tomes and parchments were opened and unrolled on a wide oak desk. Each one was in some way related to the natural world and all its wonders. From Abalone to Zebu, Air elementals to Zombies, all the creatures of the world were represented in some form or another. There, next to the lowly gaffer fish, was the mighty gagrog. A huge, thick-skinned, wide-bodied, brute of a beast. The first thing you noticed, looking at this picture, were the teeth, mighty, tree trunk sized canines jutting up from the bottom jaw like some immense bull dog's. Next were the four horns, bigger and wider if anything, standing straight up from the skull, two in front and two closer together behind, forming a seat with the lump of flesh on top of the head. She stared at the horns, imagined herself sitting there, commanding the creature to engorge entire battalions of men, impaling wizards by the score on the great teeth, crushing great holes in the enemies lines with barely a thought. Men would flock to her side, and women too, and then she would see who would be running this kingdom.

Carefully, she read the small, faded text. When she finished, she closed the book, and all the others to stop people discovering her plans, swallowed the lump in her throat and slowly left the library. This wasn't going to be as easy as she thought.

Eight

"I knew we shouldn't have come this way."

"K'treema, stop fussing, the farmer said Esh was on the edge of the Death land. All we need do is follow the edge until we find it. That's not difficult, look right, what do you see? Rock. Look left what do you see? Farmland. Right, so it's not exactly green, but there are things growing there. So, here we are, on the right track." Shemaz gestured as she spoke, finally chopping her hand along the path they were following.

"You're right Mazzy, I shouldn't fuss, but it's been a long time since we found water, and we don't know how much further it is."

"We have water though, the farmer let us fill up at his well. And all for a few of your tricks."

"That was kind of him, I'm still hungry though, all we've had is a few pieces of bread."

"K'treema, you're never satisfied," Shemaz huffed.

"And some roast meat and sun fruit."

Mazzy was about to scold K'treema when she noticed her friend trying not to smile. "You old trickster." Shemaz grabbed K'treema's long plait and tugged sharply.

"Ouch, that hurt." K'treema laughed, turning around. "I'll light your backpack in a second, then we can have that for supper."

Laughter died in their mouths as the sound of horses clattering on the firm ground reached their ears. They had been following an old trade route that wound its way through the borderlands. The ground was solid here and never churned into mud when the rains came, but was near enough to water to allow the traders to drink on the long journey. The track followed the line of least resistance and dipped and turned around boulders and rocky outcrops, causing visibility to diminish to only several yards in places. K'treema and Shemaz realised they were in just such a dip when the first horses rounded the corner in front of them.

Expecting an army patrol, the two were completely unready for the sight that greeted them. Nine riders appeared, an assortment of men on a range of horses, none exactly alike, and all armed to the teeth, quite literally in some cases.

They stopped at the sight of the two women, grinning widely.

"Well, well, and well. What have we here? Two fine ladies, travelling alone and unaccompanied, and in such a dangerous place too, as well. Why don't you let us look after you for a while, and take care of you?"

The men laughed, some through teeth gritted into half round metal disks that looked very sharp.

"We are wizards, travelling on our Journey. We may not be harmed by order of the emperor. Now leave us in peace or we will teach you a lesson." Shemaz stood defiant, hoping her bluff would deter them.

"Well, well, and well. Aren't you a pretty one my beauty, when you are all angered up and enraged? But 'scuse me, pretty, and pardon me, but I don't see no emperor, or his pretty little pussycats anywhere. So stop your whining and show me what you got."

Shemaz froze, now they were in trouble. She backed away a step, moving protectively towards K'treema. Risking a glance to check on her friend, she was completely startled to see her drawing her power. She had seen that look of concentration before, when K'treema had earned their water. What was she doing?

For answer, the leader suddenly flew backwards, as if punched from his horse. Shemaz was suddenly terrified, what had she done? K'treema had believed her bluff even if the men hadn't. Now she was starting something they couldn't possibly finish.

Well, there was only one thing for it, Shemaz thought as another man went rolling backwards. Fight, fight with all they had. Another roll of terror engulfed her as she realised she didn't have anything, just a few ribbons of wind.

The men had quickly recovered and were approaching the wizards on foot, there were too many for K'treema to deal with alone, she would have to do something.

Finding the warm spot she had discovered on the ship, Mazzy de-focused on her surroundings and concentrated on the wispy ribbons that eddied around the rocks. She found a small whirlwind and began whipping it up faster. Then, barely controlling it, she directed it at the raiders.

It was small, too small and too weak to do any damage, but it picked up loose grit and threw it into the men's faces. Momentarily, they backed away, rubbing their eyes and cursing. Another one was knocked off his horse by K'treema's power, but he too got up madder than ever.

Having no option now but to continue, Shemaz and K'treema struggled on. The whirlwind got slowly bigger and faster, but K'treema was tiring and the men were barely feeling her punches.

Shemaz concentrated, desperate to at least hold the men off, there was a chance someone would arrive, and this was a trade route. But then these men weren't fools; they had probably scouted out the whole area.

With one last push, Shemaz drove the whirlwind as hard as she could at the men, if she could blind them, then she and K'treema could run away. The whirling dust devil quickened slightly, but sapped Shemaz's strength. She saw the ribbons of air begin to unwind. Despite her heart-rending effort, her body began to lose its power.

K'treema too was tiring, there was only so much energy in the human body, and she had used most of it up. Her last punch formed in her head, a small fist, like a child's, hardly about to do any damage to a stout warrior. This is it, she thought in the back of her mind; this is where I find out what sex is like. Not quite how she had imagined her first time.

Nine

It was an unmistakable feeling. Like a tingling in his mind, as though his brain itched. Someone was using magic, somewhere very close by. Dhomag turned slowly until the itch was strongest, and then set out to find the source.

The mage had travelled across the lands called Death in an uncannily straight line; stopping briefly when he reached the cave he had emerged from. He had taken a moment to study the cave, and to reflect on his former life, a life only revealed to him in flashes of brightly hued pictures.

There had been a woman, hair so long she could sit on it. He didn't know who she was. Bushes, long rows of plants bearing fat, juicy fruits. And an animal, four legs and covered in fur. Then other men came and took him away, locked him in a dark hole, not a cave, but lined with stone. Then, suddenly, he was under a bright light, fire burning on his flesh.

Nothing more. At least not yet. But one thought remained, a thought so strong, but ironically had no picture. I am Dhomag, and I have sworn to kill the emperor.

The other men, soldiers of some kind – it was strange how he could still speak, and knew the words for rocks and clothes and swords – had told him to go east, so that's what he had done. Heading for the nearest town, and a long awaited drink of water.

A noise, heard and felt, reached him from just over the boulder before him. Instead of walking straight in, only to have to kill them all again, he lay against the boulder and willed himself up its smooth side, stopping just in sight of the ensuing fight.

Two young women, hardly more than girls, where holding off a group of determined men. Their puny magic fizzed and burped around like a bunch of children at play. The men were getting closer, hampered by a tiny whirlwind, generated from within by the blonde haired girl. She would never keep that up for any length of time. And the one with darker hair was doing just as badly. Dhomag could feel the magic pictures forming in her head, then being popped out by her force of will, which was getting more and more feeble.

The mage didn't really understand magic; he merely felt it surge through him when he called it. But as these two where obviously like him, at least to a degree, he decided to help. Besides, they were both quite pretty; he needed a closer look to decide which he liked best. Perhaps he would have them both.

From deep within the rock on which he lay, Dhomag channelled the power of the earth into a towering ball of energy. It seethed and burned like a mighty storm trapped in a small space. One finger lined up on the men, who remained oblivious to the body shattering force about to be unleashed on them.

The two wizards stood side by side, they would fight with their fists until their strength was drained if they had to. They understood that the fight would be futile, but perhaps they could do a little token damage to these thugs.

The whirlwind quickened, expanded in size and power. Quite suddenly instead of lifting dust, it was lifting men, spinning them around like tops. The whirlwind swallowed another man, smashed him into the first, and then threw them both side ways, crashing them into the gully walls. With sickening thuds, the men bounced, and then lay still in crumpled heaps.

K'treema looked at Mazzy wide eyed, then let the last of her energy go at the leader, who was standing amazed, trying to rub his eyes to see if what he thought he saw was real. The fist that K'treema had imagined flew towards him as she released it. The image smashed into him like a tree trunk, knocking him over the other men and sending him impacting into a rock. The sound of cracking bones filled the sudden silence.

Then there was a mad scramble as the other men, seeing three bodies crushed almost boneless, dived on their horses and dashed back the way they had come.

Shemaz and K'treema stood alone in the silent gully, frozen in the positions they had been in whilst using their magic. Slowly, K'treema uncurled her fist and dropped her arms to her side. Shemaz relaxed her flattened hands, her tensed shoulders, and gritted her teeth. The two looked at one another. Wide eyes slowly creased as broad smiles filled their faces. Laughter went echoing off the rock walls. Abruptly they stopped, looked askance at the bloody corpses, and walked away. When they were out of sight, they laughed again, whooping and shouting.

"How did we do that? What a great thrill that was," K'treema enthused.

Shemaz agreed. "Yes, I wager that was better than sex."

"I'll tell you later," K'treema giggled.

They set off again, spirits high, the occasional ribald comment sending peels of laughter over the sparse landscape.

When they had calmed down they fell silent for a while, each getting straight in their mind the events of the day.

K'treema was relieved, she had known her magic wasn't very strong, but then not many wizards were. She had thought herself capable of looking after herself though. Obviously she had a lot to learn. But that was precisely why wizards went on their Journeys, to learn. And she was only young; there was plenty of time. She just had to stay alive.

Shemaz had received another boost of confidence. Her magic was there for her when she needed it. So yes, it was a little specific; she would just have to be imaginative with the using of it. They had defeated the raiders, driven them off, and taught them a little respect for wizards. All in all a good day, now all she needed was a good night's sleep.

It was K'treema who saw him first, a tall, lone male who appeared out of nowhere, the heat haze shimmering him into existence from nothing. The man stood, just to one side of the track, waiting.

"Do you think he's one of the raiders?" K'treema asked.

"Doesn't look like one, but you can never be sure, best we prepare in case he is," Shemaz answered, steeling herself, shoulders back, head high.

"I don't think I've got anything left," K'treema sighed.

"Me neither, but he doesn't know that. We'll bluff it out, like before."

"It didn't work before," K'treema squeaked a little too loudly.

"Oh, let's hope this guy is a bit more gullible then."

Trying to look braver than they felt, the two wizards walked on, looking ahead, trying to ignore the man. When they drew level, the man took a step forward, a wide smile on his face.

Both wizards did their best to ignore him, but their eyes where drawn irresistibly to him. Their eyes met, two on two, then two more. Both young women felt their hearts skip a beat, their heads whirl, their awakening libido blossom. For here was the most handsome man they had ever seen. Sandy hair crowned his head, his sharp blue eyes liquid in the bright light. When he smiled, his white teeth rivalled the sun for brightness. Broad shoulders gave to a broad chest, barely covered by a linen tunic. His waist narrowed just enough, then barely swelled over firm buttocks. A long, thick bulge under leather trousers, that snagged both girls eyes for several seconds, separated his long, muscular legs their mouths slowly drooping open. Even his feet were nice, perfectly formed and strong in leather sandals. And that bulge.

The man spoke. His voice a deep, throbbing rumble that set their bodies tingling. He spoke again before the women dragged their eyes from his trouser front and back to his face.

"Shy are you? Where are you headed?"

"We, er, we are headed for Esh, along the route here," Mazzy stumbled.

"Yes, we're wizards, we're on our Journey, you know, to learn things." K'treema blushed, she sounded so stupid.

"No, I didn't know, do all wizards Journey?"

"Oh yes, it's part of the training."

"Yes, it helps to teach, well, you tell him," they both answered.

"And are all wizards as pretty as you two?"

"No. Not that I think I'm pretty. K'treema is though."

"Well, I wouldn't say that, I think Shemaz is the pretty one." The two girls nudged each other, both blushing furiously.

"And this Esh, does it lead to wherever the emperor is?"

"The emperor? Well, he's probably in Oq, that's the capital. It's on the main road from Esh. Or actually Esh is on the main road from Oq. Why, do you need to speak with him? I've heard he's very wise, and quite generous,"

Shemaz said, smiling sweetly.

"I'm going to kill him, nail him to a rock probably."

The two wizards looked at each other, their faces wide with astonishment. Then they laughed. "You nearly fooled us then," Shemaz said.

"I thought you meant it," K'treema giggled nervously.

"Oh, I do," the mage said. "I have vowed to destroy the emperor for what he did to me."

K'treema and Shemaz casually moved backwards, half a step at a time. "What did the emperor do to you?" Mazzy asked.

"I don't remember everything, but he certainly nailed me to a rock. And he did something terrible before I died, for which I swore vengeance, so even though I can't remember, he's still going to die, as slowly as I can manage."

Despite the almost physical power of his charisma, K'treema and Shemaz began to move away. Typical, K'treema thought, what a stallion, and weak in the head.

"There's no need to be afraid, I won't hurt you, it's only the emperor, and perhaps a few hundred of his cowardly, stinking soldiers. You're quite safe. Besides, I've already saved your lives once today."

The two wizards stopped and chorused, "You did?"

"Yes, back there in the gully. You don't think that was you doing that did you? Your puny little efforts wouldn't strip paint off a door. I was going to melt the bastards, but I thought you'd appreciate it better if I just assisted your little efforts. I wasn't sure if you'd like all that blood, I don't personally, so messy. Where are you going?"

K'treema and Shemaz linked arms, turned and set off along the trail. "Did you hear that, 'Ttreem? Calling our magic puny? We'll show him a thing or two, when we've rested."

"Yes, Mazzy, I don't think we need to stay around here much longer, not a lot to learn here. I think he's been out in the sun too long."

After a couple of minutes of silence, they turned around to find the trail, and the landscape beyond, devoid of men. They were a little worried, but when he didn't re-appear, they set off at a brisk walk, planning an early night at the first shady spot they came across.

Dhomag was puzzled by the women's behaviour, but he had to admit he wasn't exactly skilled at these things. He decided to follow along a little behind, just to study them of course. As he walked, about ten paces behind, he concentrated on being unobtrusive, he didn't want to upset them again.

Ten

Bright lanterns cast pools of white light along the palace walls. In between, areas of darkness sat, small, but just about big enough to hide a princess. With her intimate knowledge of the palace and its guards, Oleana-tarli had easily evaded her ladies in waiting, the upstairs servants, the downstairs servants, and the royal bodyguard.

Out here was a different matter, there were several ways out of the actual palace, but only three exits from the palace walls. The main gate was out of the question, too many well-known faces; half her ex-guards were stationed there, finally relieved of latrine duty. The third gate was for tradesmen and deliveries, and sometimes prisoners, so she would never go that way.

Which only left the second gate, smaller, used by people on foot to avoid the animals and their produce around the main gate. Tonight, more than ever, there were guards everywhere. The king's war plans were in full swing, and he was a little paranoid about spies. Oleana-tarli waited until the two guards who would see her turned away, something that happened about every two minutes, then she ran through the light, to stop, her heart pounding, in the next concealing shadow. Twice more she moved, both times managing to be hidden before a guard appeared.

Finally, she approached as near the gates as she dared. A ring of soldiers stood across the gateway. Her heart sank; there was no chance of getting through that lot. What a waste of effort she thought, all that planning: Secreting small amounts of food in a leather pack she had acquired from a servant, borrowing plain clothes from her ladies whilst they were out, getting a pair of stout boots that fit her, and worst of all, having to wear all this stuff, second hand, drab, not a single jewel in sight. And the slight odour of someone else's body.

No! She forced herself to think of something else, vomiting now would only give her away. Think of the soft silk underwear caressing my inner thighs, she pictured in her mind. Think of the large ruby pendant hung on a gold chain snuggled between my firm breasts. Laughter brought her back to the present. The guards were moving away, down the tunnel in which the gate sat. The sound of hoof beats reached her shortly after.

Quickly, Oleana-tarli moved over to the edge of the gate, stopping inside one of the shallow guard's boxes. It smelled of leather and men, of sweat and warm bread. She didn't know whether to puke or smile. Instead she peered around the edge of the wooden structure and watched the soldiers.

A large wagon had been dragged up the hill by four large horses. The back of the wagon was covered over with a piece of off-white cloth. The soldiers had surrounded the wagon and were searching it thoroughly. Although they had their backs turned, any attempt to get past would have met with failure. There was just too many of them and too little space.

The wagon, after much complaining by the driver, was turned around and sent away, whether to the rear gate or the main gate, where it should have been, Oleana-tarli didn't know. Then suddenly she had an idea, as she wasn't going to get out tonight anyway, she would risk all on a long shot. Besides, what would her father do if he caught her trying to get out? Lock her in her room probably, with all that jewellery and fine clothes, and all those guards to play with. She would stay for a while then simply try again, her father was such a trusting soul. It would come as something of a shock when she rode the gagrog into his bed chamber and stole his crown, right from under his mistress's buttocks.

The princess gathered herself together, pulling the hood of the travelling cape around her face. She had taken the precaution of dying her well-renowned and much admired long black hair a shade of red. It had pained her, probably more than anything else, but it had to be done, she would show off her black locks all the time when she was queen. Probably pass a law demanding that all other girls with black hair dye it or have it shaved off. Or lose their heads. She almost laughed out loud, managing to stop herself just in time.

Sneaking quietly along the shadows, she approached the soldiers, who were spread out across the gateway watching the cart. Then she moved into the light and turned around, facing back into the palace. When nothing happened, she was forced to pretend to slip to attract the attention of the guards.

"Hey! How did you get in here?" One of them shouted.

There was a rush of stomping boots and several guards surrounded her. One of them stepped forward and grabbed her arm. "And where do you think you're going, traveller? The king doesn't want any more visitors today."

Oleana-tarli was furious, no one touched the royal person without permission. She glared at the soldier, and before she could stop herself she screeched. "I am the princess Oleana-tarli, unhand my person at once."

The guards roared with laughter. "We do apologise your ladyship, we didn't recognise you, what with your flowing black hair, famed across the land, all covered up."

"Well, famed across the land when the princess is about anyway, I've seen horses with shinier hair than hers." They laughed again. One of the soldiers grabbed her hood from behind and pulled it back, taking some of her hair with it. She squealed, and although she fumed like a miniature furness inside, years spent with a governess allowed her to control herself.

Wisps of hair, obviously red in the quickly produced lantern, set the soldiers to laughing again. "Well, my dear, it seems you are a princess, why don't you come around to my house tonight and treat me like a prince?" The man moved in close, pushing his body against her. From behind, another guard pushed her forwards. "If you don't unhand me and let me go immediately, the King shall hear of this, and believe me, I'm closer to him than you think."

The guards looked at one another, and lacking a senior officer to hide behind, they all moved two paces backwards. "All's well lady, don't get all knotted up. You can go on your way," one of them said, holding out his empty hands. The princess, ruffled and blushing walked off back into the palace, meaning to have a very long bath, and change out of these smelly clothes.

"Er, miss? This way." A soldier grabbed her shoulder and turned her around. "The king's busy, remember?" The guards laughed again, but only quietly. Oleana-tarli, dazed but suddenly triumphant, walked out of the palace gates and into the city beyond. "One up for the women's team I think." she whispered as she descended the hill.

Once into the quiet of the city of Iamun, Oleana-tarli was almost free to go wherever she chose. Provided you had coin, which was hardly a problem to a princess, almost anything was for sale. The only problem she had now was who to trust. She knew where the gagrog would be, the books had told her it lived in warm swampy places. The only location where it was warm and swampy was to the north, in the lands of the Okovon. Getting there was easy. After all, the swamps lay within the kingdom of Iamunaya, and therefore under her father's rule. He was a soft old thing; she had to admit, a bit like the swamp really. Warm and soft, a little foggy at times, and prone to offensive odours. Still, a swamp was a dangerous place if underestimated, the King too was known to catch out the unwary, and make them disappear into the foetid depths of the palace.

Another quandary then, travel alone and keep the secret of the gagrog all to herself, but risk being robbed or captured by a greedy merchant and made to dance covered in nothing but oil in front of his customers. I really must try and concentrate, she thought; keep my mind on the task.

So, she reasoned, travel with a merchant, as a fare-paying passenger, keep my independence, but still have some degree of security. Good, that should work. Now, let's find a caravan that's going north.

Eleven

The two wizards had found a small village just before nightfall, and despite keeping a watch from the small barn they had been allowed to rent, they completely failed to notice Dhomag walking in and entering the one tavern. He had watched them from a hundred paces back, and had seen them go into the tavern, come out and enter the barn, a pitcher of something and a basket of what smelled like warm bread between them.

The tavern, more a room in someone's house, was completely silent apart from a pitiful fire smouldering in the blackened grate. Dhomag moved over to it and increased it a little, stretching his hands out to warm himself. He didn't know why, he never felt cold, nor hot, or thirsty for that matter. He did remember once being dry, almost too dry to be alive, but the memory faded as he watched the flames dancing.

A woman entered, stopping short when she saw him. "Oh, please forgive me sir, I didn't hear you come in, and Boko there usually makes such a fuss when guests come in." The woman, middle aged, thin but nicely curved, had long, straw like hair, tied back with a red scarf. Her brown eyes where kindly and moved constantly up to Dhomag's face and away again. She indicated a small dog, well muscled and capable of defending its mistress at need.

The dog, with the wisdom of its kind, had nothing but nice things to say about the guest, who was welcome to come and go anytime, without a whine or whimper from him.

"I've no beds left sir, just let the barn, too. But you're welcome to bed down in front of the fire if you wish. And we do a lovely supper, roast chicken, specially cooked for you." She smiled, encouraging Dhomag for the right answer.

"Yes, that sounds good, and water."

"Water sir? We've got a good ale, if you'd prefer, my fella makes it, very well thought of around here."

"Yes, that sounds nice." Dhomag couldn't remember what he liked to eat, or drink, but none of it brought back bad memories, so he thought he'd give it a go.

In the barn, the two wizards had settled down in low hammocks after eating their bread and chicken, washed down with cold water. They spoke a little of their respective lives up until that point, then drifted off into a deep sleep.

They were awakened in the late dawn by shouting. It seemed the woman in the tavern was having trouble with a customer. K'treema and Shemaz gathered up their belongings and went to investigate.

An altercation was taking place on the step of the tavern, a large man was saying something quietly to a woman, who was trying to control herself, but was getting louder as she argued.

"Oh no!" Groaned Mazzy, "It's him, the sun baked brain from the trail."

Dhomag turned around. All suddenly fell quiet as Dhomag smiled, a broad flowing grin that seemed to out shine the sun. The two wizards felt their hearts racing; the tavern keeper fell silent, almost physically. The few early rises stopped in their tracks, mouths fell open, and hearts skipped a beat. "Ladies, it seems I have forgotten to bring any money, could you see your way to advancing me a few coins?" He asked quite reasonably. Everyone gathered there, including the tavern keeper, reached into their purses, bags and money belts, pulling out random coins and offering them to Dhomag. He took a few of the ones offered by K'treema, as she was closest, and gave them to the woman. She blushed a royal red and stumbled back inside.

Dhomag returned his attention to Ktreema and Shemaz. "I am in your debt, it seems, allow me to travel with you, maybe I can make it up to you in some other way."

"Yes, of course, we would like that," K'treema breathed.

Shemaz stood quietly, something nagging at the back of her mind, but she couldn't remember what. All she could feel was the beating of her heart and the pulse between her legs.

Dhomag reached out both hands and fingered the necklaces the wizards wore. "These are very pretty, very well made. They suit you, set off the colour of your eyes."

Both women blushed pink, mumbling a thank you.

"Well, as you appear ready, and I travel light, let's go." Dhomag strode off, K'treema and Shemaz close behind.

Once out of the village, Dhomag relaxed, he thought he had handled that quite well, all he had needed to do was be polite, and everyone was his friend.

Shemaz strode across the dry land, the breeze clearing her head. "Wait a minute." She stopped. "What are we doing going with him? He said our magic was puny. Come on 'Tree, let's show him what we can do."

K'treema stopped a few paces ahead of her friend, shaking her head in confusion. "What's happening here? And who the dung are you?"

"I told you, I am Dhomag, and I saved you back there."

"Like dung you did, we saved ourselves with magic, we'll show you," Mazzy yelled.

They stood side-by-side, heads relaxed forwards and eyes unfocused. Dhomag felt a warm glow begin to expand inside each woman, then a flow of power as they released their magic. A whirlwind grew from the breeze, picking up sand and bits of dry twig. A sudden slam blasted into the sand beside the whirlwind, kicking up stones and lumps of soil. Dhomag looked over at the wizards to find them smiling, lines of strain on their foreheads, beads of sweat just forming. He lifted his little finger and quashed the whirlwind, flattening it to nothing, stopping the air with such force a boom sounded. Shemaz stumbled forward, as though the whirlwind had been holding her up. K'treema steadied her. "Hey, be careful! You could have hurt her, don't you know you shouldn't cross magic?"

"Sod that," said Shemaz, "I want to know how he did it, I've never seen such power. Boom! Just like that, no time, no sweat." She turned accusingly to Dhomag, "How did you do that?"

He shrugged, "it was easy, I just sort of channel it, and out it comes."

"Easy for you maybe, we've been studying for years, and have years to go before we even get anywhere near that." Shemaz pointed at the spot where the whirlwind had died. "Perhaps you can teach us? We'll let you travel with us, and in turn we learn from you." She turned to K'treema for confirmation. K'treema nodded. "Imagine returning from our Journey with power like that? The young wizards would all be clambering to find out where we've been." She laughed, eyes bright.

"It's a deal." Mazzy held out her hand towards Dhomag. He looked at it, but felt no magic in there. Finally he took it, shaking it lightly, and then bringing it to his lips. Shemaz trembled all over as his lips touched. Next K'treema did the same, also receiving a kiss that coursed all the way up her arm and down her spine.   And so they set off, three wizards together.

That night they walked until it was almost dark looking for a place to stop, but found only bare ground and a few scrubby trees. They were about to settle under one of them when Dhomag noticed a glow between the rocks just off the trail towards the west. The three decided to go and have a look, and if it turned out to be traders or travellers, they would ask to join them.

Moving quietly, they traversed along the flat ground

until they could see the light from several fires burning in a row along the bottom of a ravine. Five or six figures sat or lounged around each fire, silhouetted or lit by the dancing flames.

Shemaz and K'treema gasped, dropping down to the ground. Dhomag looked around. "What?" he said. K'treema grabbed his belt and pulled him down. "Look," she hissed, pointing to the nearest fire, "On their armour, the symbol of the king of Iamunaya."

"Is that bad?" Dhomag asked although he knew the symbol, the men who had last worn it had proved no trouble at all.

K'treema and Shemaz looked at each other wide-eyed. "Don't you know? Iamunaya declared war on the Empire years ago." K'treema hissed. "And got soundly beaten. What are these soldiers doing on this side of the Death lands?"

Mazzy turned up her palms. "Don't know, but I don't like it. Someone ought to warn our soldiers."

"Right." K'treema agreed.

"Well, there are only a few of them, and we are wizards, why don't we just go and deal with them." With that Dhomag stood and walked towards the campfires.

"Stop you idiot, we don't have the power to deal with that many...oh damn he's not listening. What should we do Maz? Someone's got to warn the emperor."

"You're right K'treema. And I think I know just the two wizards for the job. But let's just see how the good-looking man with the empty head gets slaughtered." Shemaz lowered herself as far as she could and still see.

"Shemaz! That's terrible." But K'treema too laid down to watch.

Familiar warmth grew inside Dhomag as he walked, drawing up power from the rocks. At a certain level, he experienced the feeling of connection, as though he were tapped directly into the ground.

After only a few strides he was within sight of the camp and was soon spotted by a sentry. A voice called out, "Halt, drop your weapons and walk slowly forwards or be treated as foe."

Dhomag wasn't sure of the language, wasn't even sure he had heard the separate words, but he somehow knew their meaning. The power within surged along his arm and a small ball of energy popped from his fingertip. Before the guard could cry a warning a hole appeared in his throat. A strangled gurgle sounded, then the thump of armour on rock. The noise roused soldiers standing nearby, who leapt up, fumbling for weapons and shouting an alert.

Dhomag's heart began to beat faster, his body strained with welled up power, a smile crept unbidden across his face. Three more soldiers went down, smoking holes through armour and chest. From behind the first fire, the slap of several crossbow strings sounded, bolts screamed towards him. Something inside him clicked, his heart rate increased, as though he had stepped up a speed. The quarrels came towards him, like hornets, like birds, like butterflies. Casually he picked them out of the air, burned them to ash in his hands, and then crushed the ash to dust.

Still the soldiers came, the front row pushed from behind by those who had not yet witnessed his power. Weapons were raised, swords and spears, maces and long bladed axes, a forest of sharp metal dashing towards him. The mage watched it all with calm interest. Soldiers approached on three sides with deadly intent, but running like they were in water. Hands raised, Dhomag gestured towards the men, palms out. Energy rushed forth, up his legs, through his torso and along his arms. A wall of fire ignited right before the rushing mass, but no ordinary fire. As the soldiers impacted with it they stopped as though hitting stonewall.

* * * * *

The ones at the front died instantly, those behind receiving varying degrees of injury. The attack stopped. Half the force was dead or injured. An order for withdrawal was shouted from the back, the soldiers turned and ran, happy to comply.

But the wall moved with them, burning and crushing as it went, finishing off the injured, chasing down the retreat, turning it to rout.

Dhomag walked with it, guiding the fire as it pushed along the ravine. A few of the braver men tried to fire through it, but the bolts burned well before they hit the wall.

A strange itching sensation caught Dhomag's attention. Turning, he noticed a soldier rise up from behind a boulder to one side of the ravine, partly sheltered from the fire. Although the man's hair was burned away and his armour was still smouldering, he sighted carefully along his crossbow and squeezed the trigger.

The hornet neared Dhomag, then stopped in mid air. It caught fire, burning with an intense blue flame. Then it flew backwards, crashing fletchings first into the soldier's skull. The soldier dropped over the boulder, crossbow still gripped. And the wall never faulted.

At the end of the shallow ravine, the wall narrowed. The surviving soldiers were scrambling up and out, dashing away into the land called Death, preferring to face the desert than the burning, crushing wall.

As the last of them reached the top, Dhomag stopped the wall and removed the magic, channelling it back into the rock. In no particular hurry, he scaled the rocky slope and studied the men as they scattered. Suddenly, he raised both hands and shot globes of energy at four of the men in quick succession. All four men went down, neat holes letting the last of the light through their skulls. Another man ran on, his footsteps thumping into the distance. Dhomag raised his arm.

"Wait," a voice said breathlessly, "Wait, we need one alive, to ask him questions." K'treema gasped. Dhomag turned to her and smiled, "Sorry." he said, and then looked down at his feet, lips tight with regret.

"What?" K'treema asked, looking at the rapidly disappearing man. She was about to turn around and check on Shemaz when something impacted into the soldier, turning a full sized adult male into an expanding cloud of body parts, each no bigger than a hen's egg. Apart from his boots and the bottom part of his calfs, which flopped over intact.

Shemaz came running up behind, and looked in the same direction as K'treema. "What are we looking at?" She asked.

"Just think yourself lucky it's dark Mazzy, that's all I'm going to say." She turned away and walked back down into the ravine.

Shemaz looked at Dhomag, who was standing somewhat contrite, and looking nowhere in particular.

"Did we not get one alive then?" She asked.

"No, I didn't realise you wanted one alive. You could have had them all if you'd told me." Dhomag shrugged and walked away.

K'treema and Shemaz stepped carefully along the gully, examining Dhomag's work.

"There's no blood," K'treema remarked, "Look, not a drop. Every wound burned closed, like the healers do sometimes. And where did he get all that power, he must be exhausted?"

They both looked around together. Dhomag was at the other end of the gully, lifting up the bodies and throwing them onto a pile some thirty paces away.

"So much for that theory," Shemaz sighed, "I wonder if he'll teach us how to do that?"

"Well, we could ask. You know, he's almost as powerful as those mages we read about."

The two wizards froze, and then slowly their glances met. Two pairs of eyes widened, then turned to watch Dhomag, who was rapidly reducing the bodies to ash with various sized and coloured fireballs.

After a while, once they had got control of their lower jaws, the two sat on a boulder. "He can't be, that was a thousand and a hundred years ago, he doesn't look much over, what three hundred and fifty." Shemaz giggled.

"Be serious, Shemaz. We may have a full-blown mage on our hands. Besides, those olden mages had power to regenerate themselves, make themselves look younger. And how else do you explain the power? There's no way my teacher could summon enough energy to even create that wall of fire he did, never mind keep it going that long. No, I think he's getting his power from his surroundings, leaching the goodness from the soil to feed his ghastly spells."

Shemaz looked at K'treema, then at the surrounding desert. "What soil? There's nothing alive around here for days, except idiots like us and the odd hairy arsed mage."

"Yes, but...how do you know he's got a hairy backside?" K'treema bristled, just a little jealously.

"I don't, it's just something we used to say about wizards in my village, I don't know why. I'll tell you later." Shemaz grinned.

"Shemaz! The man might be a mage, how could you stand to even go near him never mind, you know, with him?"

"Look, if he is a mage, and I can see many ways in which a mage, when threatened by the great destruction of magic all those years ago, could have protected himself, not least by using magic, where was I? Oh yes, if he is a mage, what can we do about it? Two wizards in training, two virgins with all the power of a small whirlwind and a smack in the teeth. Great chance we'd stand. What we need to do is follow him, learn his intentions and even some of his tricks, then take it from there. Perhaps even inform the emperor, get him to send his best wizards along."

K'treema had blushed slightly at the virgins remark, but had now gathered herself. "Surely we don't want to learn his power? Strip the land of goodness just to fling a few spells? No thanks, we'd get lynched."

"I think it was 'cast', they cast spells not flung them.

Besides, I'm not suggesting we use his methods, but if we could learn to focus power like he does with those fire things he pops out of his fingers, that would be something to show off when we got back." Shemaz looked pleadingly at K'treema.

"Well, provided things don't start to die as we travel, and you promise to keep out of his bed roll, I think we'll be fine."

"I never said I wanted to share his bed roll, besides, I don't think he's got one, a bed roll that is. And he's not exactly smart is he, a bit slow on the old worldly things."

"He has been away a long time, think how much the world has changed since. Imagine having to go and hunt food everyday, and not having clothes to wear. Terrible."

"I think they had clothes, Tree, just not nice ones."

"Well, yes I suppose they did, but they must have been really smelly, all those furs and hides, ugh."

"He's coming over, talk about something else."

Both women smiled inanely as Dhomag approached, his grisly practice session finished, the pile reduced to wind blown ash.

"I'm sorry about the man, I didn't realise you wanted to ask questions. I have checked on the others, but they were all dead. I hope you aren't too angry." He smiled, a wide, beaming lantern of white fire that burned through the wizards' anger and fear like his magic had burned the soldiers.

"It's just that, well, we are at war with them and it would have been nice to ask a question or two about their intentions and things." K'treema said gently. "But no harm done I suppose, you have probably stopped an invasion single handedly."

"Well that's good then, come on, let's camp for the night, have a little supper and you can tell me all about yourselves."

Dhomag walked away through the darkness. A few seconds later his voice called out, "Are you coming then? Have I upset you?"

"No, it's just that we can't see." Shemaz stated.

"Oh, can't you? Well, how about a little light?"

"That would be good."

A ball of white energy appeared above Dhomag's head. It rose into the air, lighting the desert for several hundred yards, almost blinding the two wizards.

"That's just a little too much, could you lower it a little?"

The light dimmed until it merely rivalled the full moon for brightness. "A touch more, if you could."

Again it dimmed, until it resembled a large lantern, the type used in palaces and castles. "That's fine." Shemaz said, and as an aside to K'treema, "After all, if he does attract any attention, who's bothered?"

K'treema laughed, taking Shemaz's arm and walking off after the floating light.

In a hole three or four hundred yards away, Falco Tarm cowered once again from the searing magic of the mage. He had skipped out of the ravine at the first sound of those popping fire balls, and ran like fury until he had fell into this hole that smelled of animal dung. He didn't care, it smelled like paradise to him, warm, safe, and away from that mad man. Orders or not, he wasn't going near that mage until he was in a crowd of people, and even then he would have to see.

When all was again quiet, Falco began to strip, removing every badge, insignia and mark that showed him to be from Iamunaya.

Twelve

Dhomag was alone again. It wasn't something he said or did; it was just that the two wizards had gone to inform the local garrison of the presence of enemy soldiers. He had been left behind to guard the border, although he did point out that even a mage of his obvious power would find it difficult to patrol a couple of hundred miles on his own. But they had insisted, in the way women tended to, at least he thought they did. Besides, they said, a big army makes lots of noise, and you had no trouble seeing the small scouting party. So here he was walking along a dusty trade route, watching for enemy activity.

Briefly, he wondered why, he did have business to attend to, with the emperor himself. Dhomag stopped, one hand idly scratching his neck, thinking. The only answer he could come up with was that he was trying to impress two good-looking women. He shrugged, oh well, as good a reason as any. He walked on.

The sun beat down on the rock, heating it beyond the endurance of most creatures. All the sensible animals had retreated across the borderlands, deeper into the semi arid region. The dry, seared lands called Death remained barren. Except for two strange creatures, one who wasn't affected by the heat, or dryness and lack of food, and another who most definitely was, but who was also scared almost witless.

Falco Tarm had shadowed the mage since early dawn, after having searched for him all night. He had caught up with the man just as the two wizards faded into the distance along the road to Esh, a town of some size a days travel from the border. At first he had hung back, afraid of the welcome he would get. But the sun was cruel, and every minute that passed it grew hotter, burning his head and sapping the water from his blood. There was no choice, get out of the sun and lose him, or get the mage out of the sun with him.

Falco stood slowly, emerging from the thin gully that had concealed him. The mage was scanning the horizon, his eyes glittering with reflected light. Quickly Falco ducked back down, his nerve gone. Slapping his forehead at his own cowardice, he gathered his will and tried again. He stood, a little shakily and not quite upright, but sufficient for the approaching mage to see him. The man had his back to Falco, studying something interesting in the far distance.

To his shame, Falco Tarm cowered down, covering his head and cursing silently to his father for spawning such a miserable coward. The king has given you an order, he said to himself, who do you fear the most? He knew as soon as he had said it that it was a mistake. Of course he feared the mage more, the king was sat on his fat arse on his fat throne several days away, and although he wasn't absolutely sure, he was fairly certain the king couldn't turn a man to mist with one blink.

Think of your mother, he told himself, no, perhaps that wasn't a good idea, your father then, toiling all day in the bars and alleys of Iamun, trying to beg enough money to get drunk one more time. Well, sister? No, brother? Yes, if only he had one. He had a half sister, fathered by a travelling merchant whilst father was passed out in the bed beside his mother. But at least she'd earned a little money that night.

Half sister it would be then, dead these long years, killed by an exceptionally obese customer whilst trying to perform some kind of sexual act no one had managed to explain clearly to him. Umm! Well then, he would do it for himself, for his own self-esteem. He was only half way to his feet when he realised he didn't give a shit for himself.

But it was too late, his head had appeared just above the rock, and the mage was looking straight at him. Falco froze in terror, half crouched, as a voice called out. "Are you an invading army?"

Tarm was confused; it certainly wasn't the reaction he was expecting. The imbecilic nature of the question gave him a little strength, just enough to allow him to stand upright. The relief to his knees almost made him smile.

The mage was standing looking at him, a confident stance, a faint smile on his lips. "Are you an invading army?" He repeated. Falco blubbered something incoherent, not yet in control of his whole face.

"Do you need a hand?" The mage asked.

Falco, not at all sure of the genuine nature of the offer,

but rapidly running out of choices, replied, "I, er, no, er, I, er, I'll be, er, in a moment." Quickly he scrambled out of the gully and stood a few paces from the mage, the last thing he wanted was a hand up with those fingers.

"Hello, my name's Dhomag, are you lost?"

"No, I was just on my way to, er, the next village. Get a jug of ale and something to eat, get out of this sun. It's certainly a back burner today."

"Well I'll come with you then. How far is it to Err?"

For a moment Falco was puzzled, he had no idea there was a village, never mind one called Err. Then, going back over what he had said, he realised what the mage had heard. "It's not far, this way, only a bit of a walk." He hoped. "I'm Talco, Talco Farm." He winced as he said it, but it was too late now.

"Nice to meet you Talco." The mage smiled.

Falco felt a wave of warmth pass over him; his heart skipped a beat, and then began to melt. What a lovely man, I wonder if he's got a partner? He thought. With a quick mental slap and an inward grimace of disgust, he threw off the feeling and pulled himself together. This man was dangerous in more ways than one.

They wandered along the trail for a while, Dhomag asking questions and Falco answering in as few syllables as possible. After only a short walk, they came in sight of a large village spread along the trail and back towards the east. The main street was lined with taverns, boarding houses and blacksmiths, merchants' premises and all the allied trades of a stopping place for travellers. Falco sighed with relief, plenty of places to buy a drink and to seek shelter.

The soldier led the way, choosing a tavern that didn't look too pricey, and walked in as though he'd been there many times before. The bar tender smiled a welcome and came straight over as they leaned on the bar. "Yes travellers, what have you earned for yourselves today?"

Falco was about to answer when he suddenly realised, in his panic, he had spoken nothing but Iamunayan to the mage. But the man had answered him fluently, who was he? Falco stuttered, forced himself to switch to Empiric, which he had learned from a merchant friend of his mothers. "Yes, two ale, please."

"And some food if you have any, meat and bread, thank you." The mage added in perfect Empiric. Falco studied him. Where had this man come from? Was he a spycatcher, who even now was weaving a trap to catch Falco unawares? If this stranger was an agent he was very good, otherwise, the man wasn't very wise to the ways of the world. And if he was very naive, Falco would have some fun, and make a little retirement money on the side, and even retire now.

The sound of money chinking in his imaginary pocket increased Falco's bravery level substantially. "So, Dhomag, are you up for a little fun?"

"Actually, I'd better get back, I promised K'treema and Shemaz I'd guard the border whilst they went to fetch help."

Falco almost choked, but managed to turn it into a cough.

"You are dry, here, have a drink." Dhomag handed Falco his tankard of ale the tavern keeper had just poured. He took a long drink, then watched as Dhomag drained his own.

"Who are they then, friends of yours?" Falco asked as casually as he could.

"Yes, they're wizards, two very nice women. I haven't yet decided which one I'm going to pop first, perhaps I'll do them both together, they'd like that."

"Oh, if it's women you want, they have them here. Plenty of them. Just choose your type, or types, and off you go."

"Really? Well, that's good. But are they pretty and have big bulges on their chests?"

Falco laughed, "The more money you have the bigger and prettier they are."

"Oh, but I don't have any money." Dhomag sagged.

"That isn't a problem for a man of your talents, not a

problem at all." With a glint in his eye, Falco looked over to the back of the room, where a large wheel of fortune stood, promising riches with its shiny numbers, drawing eyes to itself with the clock, clock, clock, sound as it spun.

Thirteen

The caravaneer wasn't fooled for a minute by the plain garb his passenger had dressed herself in. He could tell every time she spoke that she was nobility. If he had been aware of just how noble, he would probably have refused to take her, in the politest possible way of course.

But money is money and children have a nasty habit of wanting to be fed, so he accepted her flimsy explanation, her rather more substantial payment, and said no more to anyone. At this moment, she sat comfortably in a low padded chair in the back of the lead wagon, the one he himself drove, trusting this passenger's care to none of the other drivers.

The route was wide and well marked, patrolled by the king's own and a prime target for bandits and robbers, usually in the guise of the king's own, who demanded high tolls for safe passage.

But this trip would be very profitable, the passenger's money would buy him a lot of safe passage, leaving the goods he carried as pure earnings.

The weather warmed as they proceeded north. The princess Oleana-tarli dozed fitfully in the lumpy chair, watching the back trail and the train of assorted wagons. She was quite pleased with her explanation to the caravaneer, he had believed every word of her story about a sick relative, and didn't even notice she was highborn; such was the cunning nature of her disguise.

All she had to do now was keep calm until they reached Ya-Okovo, Capital of the Okovon region, gateway and stop over for hunters and trappers who brought back the pelts of several animals to trade with the merchants from Iamun, like the ones she travelled with now.

Once there, she would secure the services of one such gentleman, find the gagrog, and ride home on the back of it, attack whatever enemy her father was fighting at the time, they looked like the empire lot in her vision, and snatch the throne from under her father's stupid fat backside. She smiled broadly, and then checked quickly that no one had seen.

Around mid afternoon a few days later the caravan came to a lurching halt. Oleana-tarli had been day dreaming again, mainly about a palace full of guards, fully armoured above the waist, totally naked below. Genitalia like root vegetables dispersed on the mental waters as reality intruded.

The driver of her wagon leaned back through the canvas and hissed, "Careful miss, there are toll men up ahead, they've stopped us to pay a toll for using this road. Just keep still and they won't bother you."

"Toll? But surely my fath…Surely this is the king's road, why do we need to pay a toll?" The princess questioned irately.

"Yes miss. But the king's a long way off, and what he don't see he don't worry about."

"But what about the soldiers, do they not patrol this area?"

"Oh yes miss, that they do. Watch it, here they come."

There was a clattering of hooves on the hard packed road, and the sound of forced joviality. The toll gatherers were talking to the wagoneer ahead. She couldn't make out what they were saying from inside the wagon, but she had sense enough to stay where she was.

Hooves thudded closer, this time stopping either side of her cart. She could see shadows swaying against the canvas, hear the horses panting, and metal clinking. Finally, a deep voice spoke. "And what are you hauling my man, and be truthful now?"

"Just a few bits of furniture sir, for an old lady, nothing

of value." The wagoneer answered, very nervously Oleana-tarli thought.

"Then you won't mind at all if I check, will you?"

"No, sir, not at all sir, and don't mind my apprentice, she's a bit simple, and DOESN'T SPEAK A LOT, and she gets nasty if she's woken up."

Inside the hot wagon, the princess took a deep breath and pictured within her mind a young serving girl, no threat to anyone, and of not much value either. This was quite difficult for her, but she loved beating men at anything, so she did her best.

The back flap was pulled open and two men peered in. Oleana-tarli was so shocked she almost let her thoughts break. They were quite clearly soldiers, and one a captain in the king's own cavalry. The men looked around the wagon, noting the items in transit, then looked briefly at the princess. The second man looked away, showing no interest, but the captain kept her gaze, a puzzled look on his face. Oleana-tarli could feel his mind searching for a match for the face he was certain he'd seen before. Quickly, she filled his mind with a sense of urgency for the task at hand. He shook his head and looked away.

"I think a quarter stallion for this one, he won't make much more this time around."

Nodding, the second man began to walk back to the driver. The captain re-mounted and moved on. The driver complained of course, but he paid up and they were soon moving again, catching up with the rest of the caravan.

Oleana-tarli relaxed, sighing with relief. It didn't always work, but mostly it did, to a greater or lesser degree. It didn't always depend on the intelligence of the person either, but seemed to be more successful on the more emotional person. Unless sex was involved, and that seemed to work every time. It was just inconvenient or downright dangerous to work sex into every encounter. She lay back, a smile of victory on her lips, another man duped.

Several days later, and no more encounters with

the king's troops, they arrived in Ya-Okovo, a rather disappointing town with a strange odour. The caravaneer was paid the balance of his fee, and the princess was soon ensconced in the best hotel in town, which was a poor substitute for the palace, but would have to do. And at least it didn't smell as much in there. A few discrete questions around the hotel by the manager secured her an appointment with one 'Marshwater' Chada, rumoured to be the best hunter in the area, and famed for his ability to drink marsh water and not get sick. Oleana-tarli controlled her revulsion and had him summoned.

He arrived late the next morning, still dressed in his hunting gear, stained and smelly from his latest trip. He was somewhat short for a famed explorer, wide of shoulder and narrow of hip. His head was topped by a mat of black hair that seemed to have forgotten how to fall, but instead stuck out horizontally in short spikes. His face was tanned, with a white line where his hat covered his head, and fairly plain. A battered hat was rolled up in his left hand; occasionally he would gesture with it, using it as a pointer. His mind was a boiling pot of emotion; lust, greed, envy, pride, fear, and others, all bubbling up one after the other, and then fading back. He would be very difficult to handle, but she did like a challenge.

"Good morning sir, come in and take refreshment." She said politely through gritted teeth.

"Thank you miss, and thank you for seeing me. What sort of game are we after? Red mink for a coat for yourself? Or is it Black Hununcu for a gift for...someone else?"

The princess hated him immediately and didn't at all look forward to spending a single minute with this leering idiot. She forced herself to endure, thinking about the glorious entry she would make on the back of the beast she hunted.

"No, sir, none of those. I seek the gagrog, if you are man enough."

Marshwater smiled, "Surely you're taking the pi..you jest miss? The gagrog has no pelt worth taking, and no meat worth eating, it has no horns or teeth with which to carve intricate items..."

"No horns? Are you sure? I was certain it had horns."

"No miss, the gagrog is a large, lumpy brown creature, which spends its day thigh deep in sh... in mud, eating plants and far...breaking wind. It doesn't do much else. Are you sure you have the name right?"

Oleana-tarli thought back to her vision, picturing the images in her mind. At the time, she had known it was a gagrog she rode, a mighty beast with large horns and vast teeth. Could there have been a mistake, perhaps it had been a dream after all? But it was so strong, so real. She slumped in her chair, only slightly, as befitted a princess. She had come this far, might as well go and have a look. "Yes, I am sure. I wish you to take me to the gagrog. I will pay you the usual fee, plus a bonus on success. We leave at first light tomorrow. Good day."

"Success? What success? You don't want to bring one back do you? That's fu...very expensive. I'll need men for that, and a swamp boat, a big one." The hunter explained as he was backed out of the door.

"No, it's just you and me, you will tell no one, either before we go or when we get back, or the bonus will not be paid. I will see you in the morning." With that she shut the door, waited for his protestations to fade, then locked it. She stripped off and stood naked in front of the closed shutters, wishing she could throw them wide and embrace the warm breeze. But no, not today, it would attract too much attention, and that was the last thing she needed. Instead, she walked over to the bathtub and climbed in, covered herself in scented oil and rubbed it thoroughly into every orifice, concentrating on the one beneath her fair pubic mound.

The next morning, after a restful night's sleep, Oleana-tarli rose and dressed herself in the plain leather gear she had brought with her. After a light breakfast of some kind of eggs and some kind of cooked meat cut into round pieces, she met Marshwater Chada at the back stairs and they set off for the quay.

Ya-Okovo sat in the bend of a muddy river like a collection of wooden turtles. The squat buildings lined the bank, all looking as though they could slip into the river at the first sign of danger. A long platform had been built along the bank, successive generations adding to it, until it resembled a giant tree with its flat branches growing out over the swamp into which the river emptied. The people of the region called it the quay, to everyone else it was a mostly dry walkway.

Oleana-tarli nodded a greeting to Chada, ignoring his outstretched hand as she climbed into his swamp boat. Carefully, she seated herself on the bench seat at the rear, underneath a thatched roof shade. In the middle of the boat sat two muddy skinned young men, each grasping a long oar. "Who are these?" the princess asked, scowling down her nose. "I said, you and me, no one else." She began to rise.

"Well, now miss, those are the rowers, and if don't have those, this ship isn't going fu...really very far. Unless you want to give me a hand?" Chada gestured to the rowing seat.

"No, that won't be necessary. I trust you have made suitable arrangements to ensure their silence? Don't expect me to pay out extra."

"Don't fret miss, these won't say a word, or they'll be in the sh...in trouble with me." He smiled at Oleana-tarli and turned towards the rowers. She wasn't sure what he did, but the men smiled behind their raised hands. She sat back and looked out across the river, she wouldn't allow a little childishness to spoil her finest moment.

After a few supplies were loaded and a chart consulted, all without a glance at the princess, Marshwater Chada shouted an order, unnecessarily in her opinion as the men were right in front of him, and the rowers began to pull on the long oars.

Out into the middle of the river they pulled, then stopped, allowing the sluggish current to carry the boat into the waiting marsh. At first, Oleana-tarli had thought the marsh would be a place of mud and shallow water and strange smells. But this close to the river the Okovon marsh was easily navigable in a boat. Soon enough the marsh began to thicken, causing the two rowers to stand up and push with the oars instead. The craft still moved along at a good rate, stirring up insects and small snakes, none of which bothered the princess, due mainly to the clever application of certain oils. She smiled slightly at the thought of applying more later, she might even let Chada watch, though of course he wouldn't realise this.

A meal stop was taken around mid day, Chada and the princess eating from a prepared basket; fine meats, again the round slices, eggs of some unknown origin, and a variety of fruits. The two rowers, whose names she wasn't told and didn't ask, ate from the swamp, catching a mix of bugs and reptiles, and a few knobbly fruits they snatched from an over-hanging tree. Oleana-tarli waited expectantly as Chada ate, wondering when he was going to live up to his name and start drinking marsh water. To her disappointment, he never touched the stuff, taking instead long pulls on a fine silver flask. She herself was served a passable wine from a stone jar, cool in the summer warmth.

The boat was soon under way again, heading who knew where into the deeper marsh. Chada seemed to be choosing the route carefully, but a tally of chosen openings between the small islands that had appeared showed him to be taking two lefts and two rights, followed by a couple of straight ons.

Oleana-tarli smiled to herself, if the gagrog wasn't found soon, this man was in trouble. And if she did find it, well, then they would see.

A shout came from one of the rowers, he was pointing and jumping about on his seat. The princess fixed her eyes on the direction he was indicating, expecting to see the great beast rise from the water at any moment. The rower continued to point as the boat was steered towards a wide island, one bank of which was bare mud. Chada seemed pleased, grinning and patting the rower on the head. As the small craft beached, he leaped out and rushed over to a pile of mud that was almost black against the reddish island. He soon came back, clambering into the boat. "You see miss," he smiled, "We'll soon have your beast, see that black pile? That's gagrog shi...gagrog droppings that is."

Fourteen

The land around gradually turned greener as they marched. The town of Esh, still a couple of days travel, was the nearest place that held a garrison, forcing K'treema and Shemaz to journey there for help. They had tried asking at a border village, but had been laughed at by the locals, who had suspected them of being out in the sun too long.

If they'd had enough money they could have bought horses, but their funds didn't stretch that far, and lowly wizards, although capable of earning a night's meal and lodgings, could hardly earn enough to buy a horse.

So, off they had set, leaving Dhomag to stop any other scouting parties. K'treema was convinced the king planned to invade, suspecting that, even now, a vast army was pushing its way across the lands called Death.

Shemaz wasn't so sure, she thought they were only a raiding party, sent to test the defences and grab what they could. Still, the presence of enemy soldiers, in whatever number, was cause for concern, and they needed to inform someone in authority.

The day was wearing on when it began to rain. Although not a rare occurrence, it was certainly unexpected, especially at this time of the year. With nowhere on the flat plains to shelter, the two wizards had to make do with a rather leaky tree to at least keep some of the rain off.

K'treema agreed to take the first watch, so Shemaz wrapped herself in her blanket and slept fitfully sitting on the ground and leaning against the smooth trunk.

She was shaken awake whilst it was still dark, "Mazzy? Wake up. Something's moving out there."

Shemaz was awake in an instant, rising smoothly and searching in the direction K'treema was looking. "There was movement, out there somewhere, then something else over there." She pointed to her left. "Then they seemed to meet together. At first I thought they were going to leave us alone, but this is the third time they've been all the way around. They've stayed just out of sight so far, but I can hear them sure enough."

The padding of large feet on the puddled ground started again, moving back and forth, then all the way around the tree.

"What are they, Can you tell?" Shemaz whispered.

"I can't be sure, but I think they are slinks."

"Slinks, aren't they small lizards?"

"No, slinks are big, like cats, but also like wolves, long bodies and very long tails, they walk very low to the ground, as though weighed down." K'treema explained. "And I think they've been known to attack small groups of travellers," she gulped.

"Oh," Shemaz said, placing her back right against the tree. "Better get right in here then. I wonder if this tree is climbable?"

"It doesn't really matter, they can climb like squirrels."

"Arse!" Shemaz hissed in awe.

Two glowing eyes appeared in the light of the half moon. The eyes studied them intently, blinked, and then disappeared.

"No choice then, 'Tree girl, get your energy warmed up, let's see if we can give them something to worry about." Shemaz pulled back her sleeves and began to concentrate.

K'treema stood beside her, feeling the solidity of the tree trunk at her back, shoulder touching her friend's, giving at least an illusion of security.

Shemaz gently released a small amount of magic,

sending a probing gust of air into the darkness. "If Dhomag were here those things would be roasting over a small fire by now."

K'treema snorted, "No, those things would be on fire now, he's not really very subtle is he?"

Shemaz laughed nervously, "You're right, and why does he make that strange popping noise when he shoots those fire balls? It's almost as if he wants to impress somebody but not make too much noise."

Four eyes came into view only a short distance away. It was almost as if the animals knew the range of human sight and kept just out of it. The eyes watched for a while then separated, one pair going right, the other left.

"I think this is it K'treema, keep your eyes open and your power ready."

Sure enough the eyes appeared shortly after, one pair fastened on either woman, one from either side. But now they were moving, running straight in towards the pair.

K'treema screamed, focusing a fist of power and projecting it with all her anger and fear. A shimmering image was created, but never had chance to form properly before it was slammed into the attacking slink. The wide eyes closed in pain and any unerringly human like cry pierced the night. The slink crashed to one side, landing in a muddy puddle, a tangle of limbs and tail. K'treema realised with a shock that the thing was already airborne when she had seen it, it must have been only a heartbeat away from her.

Shemaz was suddenly in a cold panic. K'treema had her fist magic to protect her, all she had was a small whirlwind which took a few seconds to build. It wasn't going to be enough. She tried anyway, tracking the small ribbons of the cool night breeze and tapping them into a rough circle. It wasn't easy as most of the breeze was going in the same direction. The eyes re-appeared, closing on her with frightening speed. With barely a chance to think, Shemaz pulled the blanket from her shoulders and held it before her, whilst moving her body to the side.

The blanket bulged and was torn from her grip. The snarling slink had no time to change its target and had hit the blanket where Shemaz used to be, carrying on and slamming against a hard tree instead of a soft human. The slink spat and howled as it struggled in the blanket. The material was soon shredded by the four sets of sharp claws. The slink looked up at Shemaz and launched itself at her.

In a panic, Shemaz ripped off her backpack and held it before her like a shield. Claws racked and scrapped against the rough material, pushing her back into the darkness. The slink's claws snagged in the cloth and the pack was pulled from Shemaz's hands, almost over balancing her. Letting go was the only option, or she would have been thrown to the ground, she knew better than to let that happen.

The slink battered the pack around between it claws until it stopped moving, then re-fastened its gaze on Shemaz. It leaped for her, claws extended towards her face.

Shemaz kicked out with all her strength, catching the slink in the chest as it suddenly jerked to a stop in mid air. Looking over it, Shemaz could make out K'treema just below the tree; she had grabbed the slink's tail, and was dragging it backwards.

The slink was strong, it gathered itself and planted its clawed feet. Then it turned on the new prey, easily able to turn round as its tail was longer than its body.

Shemaz saw at once what was happening; quickly she recovered the pack and began to attack the beast with all her strength. Her backpack was full mostly with clothes so wasn't much of a weapon, but it distracted the slink enough to stop it attacking K'treema. With a howl of rage, it turned back to Shemaz and slashed out with its clawed foot, slitting two long, parallel cuts in Shemaz's wrist and the back of her hand.

The stinging pain caused her to drop the pack and pull away her hand. The slink ignored the pack this time and moved towards her again. Shemaz could see K'treema concentrating, building up her power, she would have to give her time to get in a good blast, or they were both in trouble.

She kicked again, catching the slink just under the jaw. It howled, then snarled, opening its wide mouth, revealing a set of small teeth, very numerous, and very sharp. Another howl sounded, behind K'treema. The tall wizard turned quickly and slipped the power loose into the first now recovered slink. The attack caught it underneath as it sprang, sending it tumbling backwards. It landed with a splat in the wet mud, emitted a loud yowl, and then went quiet.

Shemaz gathered her own power, but instead of shaping the wind, she began to move the raindrops, pushing them into the slink's face and eyes, trying to make them heavier as they fell.

Rain was easier to guide, she found, and soon the slink was in its own rain shower, surrounded by dry air. It shook itself, wiped at its face with a wide paw, but was unable to shake off the water. It began to lurch around swatting out at random. Shemaz moved over to the tree and stood behind it, keeping the rain concentrated on the animal's face. She was pleased to find her power not lessening at all as the raindrops came faster and faster, hitting the cat like stones. Suddenly it had had enough, it took to its paws, long strides carrying it off into the night. The two wizards stood backs to the tree for a while, watching for another attack, but none came, and no more sounds were heard. They hugged and kissed each other in relief, laughing quietly to chase away the fear.

"I didn't know you could move the rain, you could have kept us dry for a while." K'treema smiled down at Shemaz, smoothing her wet hair away from her face.

"Neither did I. But when it looked at me with those horrible staring eyes I had to do something. I saw the rain moving like I do the wind, and that was that. Rain is a lot nicer than wind, a lot more obliging." Shemaz let out a loud sigh. "I hope they don't come back, I didn't like them at all."

"Me neither."

They stood in silence for a while longer, arms entwined and bodies pressed close together.

"Strange, but I don't feel at all like I usually do, you know, after." K'treema mused.

"Me neither, I could do all that again, no trouble at all. Perhaps we are getting better at it. That's what we travel for isn't it?" Shemaz answered.

"Looks like it's working then. I don't suppose we will ever be able to match Dhomag though. Then again, who would want to?"

"Not me, not if all the stories are true, anyway, you best get some sleep 'Tree, I'll watch the rest of the night. Besides I don't seem to have a blanket." Shemaz laughed softly, releasing K'treema and walking around the tree, keeping her back to its trunk and her eyes out into the darkness.

The dawn found them both fully awake, sharing the warmth of each other in the single blanket. There were no more slinks during the night, and none as the light brightened the landscape. Of the one K'treema had blasted, nothing remained but a gouge in the soft earth.

"What's happened here then? My neck itches almost all the way around. I hope I haven't caught something from this wet ground." Shemaz complained, scratching at her skin.

"Funny, mine's the same." K'treema said, scratching around her own neck. "Never mind, we can soon get a poultice from Esh, yours doesn't look too bad, how's mine?" She pulled open her tunic and lifted the necklace out of the way.

Shemaz studied her friend's skin carefully for a few moments. "Looks red, but that's all, and that's where you've been scratching it. Let's get going, the cool air might help."

Shemaz retrieved he battered pack and the remains of her blanket, and together they set off for Esh, neither wishing to spend another night in the open.

Fifteen

For the eighth time in a row, the wheel of fortune had spun and stopped on the exact number the strange pair had chosen. Despite repeated attempts at stopping the wheel with the lever at the back, the mechanism seemed to keep slipping and the man always chose right.

The tavern owner was now down several full stallions, and was beginning to get annoyed. He had been scowling at the two for some time, but it didn't seem to frighten them, especially the tall, good looking one. Something drastic had to be done, or the pile of coins on the table was going to get bigger.

Signalling for the wheel operator to stall, the owner held a hurried conversation with one of the bar staff, who hurried off to speak with three large gentlemen hanging around outside.

The men entered shortly after and made a beeline for Dhomag and Falco. A quick jostle of Falco's arm brought a protest from the foreigner. "Hey, watch what you do." he grunted.

"Why, what you going to do about it, stranger?" The man made the last word sound positively rude.

Falco thought for a moment, and then turned to Dhomag. "Listen, this is bar fight, it happens all the time, try not to kill, see. I explain later." Then he turned back and buried his fist in the new arrival's face.

The other two men rushed at Dhomag, who, following Falco's example, thumped them both in the head, one with each fist. Despite their size and obvious attributes, both men went tumbling backwards, smashing several pieces of furniture as they went. Neither of them got up.

Falco traded blows with the third man for a while, fighting for the glory of Iamunaya, if somewhat secretly. But finally, a combination of too much ale and not enough practice led to Falco being sent crashing to the floor, where he passed out under the wheel.

The man turned on Dhomag, but was too damaged by

Falco to do much good. Dhomag stepped in and hit the man in the stomach. The man lifted off his feet and flew backwards, stopping short of the real glass window by mere inches.

The owner rushed out indignantly. "Look at the damage. You'll have to pay, come on, hand it over." He held out his hand towards the pile of coins that made up their winnings.

"Well, it seems to me," said Dhomag, "That there were five people involved in this dispute, and that as they started it, they should pay up first." He smiled at the owner. "Don't you think?"

The owner went red, a rush of embarrassment swept over him. How could he think to cheat such a fine gentleman? What was the place coming to?

"Yes, of course. You help your friend, I'll see what these men have got in their pockets. Now, don't forget your winnings. There's a nice bath house down the street that does a little healing as well, perhaps you'd like to take him down there?"

Dhomag lifted Falco onto his feet and walked him out of the tavern, scooping up the money as he went. After a brisk walk in the cooler air, Falco came around. "What are we doing?" He slurred, then more sharply. "Where's the money?"

"I have the money, don't worry."

"Good. We got him good and well didn't we? He was cheating that wheel you know, had a lever on the back to stop it on the numbers no one had bet on. Deserves everything he got." Falco laughed.

Walking down the street, they past an armourers, and Falco suddenly remembered what he was supposed to be doing. "Come on, let's have a look in here, get ourselves some nice metal."

Dhomag was baffled as to why he would need a weapon, but followed his new friend, who seemed quite keen.

A young man sat on a stool in the shop, dozing

softly, leaning forwards as though he would fall off, then recovering in time. He jumped up with a startled cry when Falco spoke.

"Yes da, I'm not sleeping." The boy turned crimson when he saw the two men. "Hello sirs, what can I help you with?" he managed to ask.

"We need swords, good ones mind. For quality folk."

The boy eyed the men, measuring them for spending ability, and decided he didn't need to call his father in this case.

"Yes sir, look around, try a few." He sat down again. Not much point on wasting effort here.

Falco looked around. If this man wanted to be taken seriously when he assassinated the emperor, he would need a suitable weapon. Falco's mind skipped over the fact that Dhomag didn't really need a weapon, to admit he was in the presence of a real life, soul stealing, baby transmogrifying, devil summoning mage was far too frightening. Best to just think of him as a wizard of some skill and leave it at that. So he would need a sword. The Iamunayan's eyes fell on a long blade mounted on the wall. "Ah! Now that's more like it, we'll take it."

The boy looked to where Falco was looking, rolled his eyes and then smiled with glee. "That one is rather expensive sir."

"No matter," Falco yelled, "My friend here deserves the best." He nudged Dhomag, "Give me the coins, I'll deal with this."

Several minutes later, Dhomag and Falco left an ecstatic young man dancing around the shop holding several full stallions in payment for an average long sword and for another blade they had been trying to sell for years.

"You know, of course, where we should really go?" Falco mumbled, "Esh, they got some fine ales in Esh, and women too, so I'm told." Then of course, he thought, it's only a short ride along the main highway to Oq, site of the emperor's palace. "It's not too far, we could get a couple of fast horses. Do you ride?"

"I've never tried, but I'm sure I'll soon learn." Dhomag answered keenly.

"I've no doubt at all of that my friend, no doubt at all. But what of your young friends, are they not expecting you somewhere?" Falco inquired bluntly.

"Oh don't mind about them, they can take care of themselves, they are wizards you know. Besides, I can soon find them, any time at all." Dhomag grinned.

Clutching their new weapons, the pair went looking for entertainment of a warmer, softer nature.

Sixteen

An apparently empty boat drifted on the slight current that ran through a wide-open area somewhere in the Okovon swamp. The flat hull skimmed across red flowered water plants, disturbed leaf-sitters and coil snakes, but otherwise made no impression on the millions of eyes watching from every angle.

Up ahead a large, brown, what could only be described as a 'shape' moved almost imperceptibly through the water. Occasionally, the shape extended, as a large head lifted up and took a rumbling breath through a wide mouth. The fact that everything within range entered its throat at the same time seemed to bother it not at all.

Chada had spotted the quickly closing trail left by the shape, and ordered his men to ship oars and stop everything. Politely, he had asked the princess to crouch down on the deck so as not to disturb their quarry.

They all sat now at the front of the boat, pressed close together, observing the creature. So intent was she on her first glimpse of the mighty gagrog, Oleana-tarli almost didn't notice the stench of sweat and damp clothing.

Chada leaned over and whispered in her ear, his breath a cloud of alcohol and spiced meat. "That's it miss, that's your beast. Not worth working your bol...ti...buns off for is it?"

"Can't we get closer? I can hardly see it from here."

"We can try, but if it spots us it might try to overturn the boat. Couldn't do it of course, I built this bas...baby myself." Chada smiled proudly.

He moved back and had the rowers feed their oars out of the stern. Careful sculling soon had the boat moving faster, on a course to intercept the gagrog. Oleana-tarli's heart pounded in her stomach. This was it! This was where she cowed the mighty beast; this is where she became somebody. It was all she could do to stay quiet in the boat, when she really wanted to leap up and shout out to it.

The boat neared, slowing as the bow drew level exactly where the gagrog would surface next. Oleana-tarli leaned over the side and peered down between the water plants, waiting for the big mouth to rise up.

Incredibly slowly, like darker water flowing beneath the brown of the swamp, the beast rose, opening its cavernous maw. The boat moved towards it as the water rushed in. Plants, animals, silt, everything gurgled down into the chest as it inhaled a huge breath, sucking in the damp air as though a massive bellows had been pulled open. A moment of panic gripped Oleana-tarli as her perspective changed, the opening loomed large before her, filled her view. She steadied herself, if she was to master the creature she had to get used to these things.

As slowly as it had emerged, the brown shape with the tiny eyes, and yes, she had to admit, no visible teeth or horns, sank back into the swamp, hardly a ripple disturbed the calm. The rest of the animal flowed under the boat, taking quite a time to pass. The crew, and Chada, despite his earlier confidence, hung tightly to the side rail until the beast was well past.

"Well miss, not very impressive ay? Just a large bag of pi...water and not much else." Chada remarked when he had recovered sufficiently.

"No, I must admit, not what I was expecting." Oleana-tarli hung her head; perhaps it had been a dream after all.

"We can see if we can find another, if you like?" Chada offered.

The princess lifted her head. "What, there are more?"

"Oh yes, not many, they are quite rare. They aren't often seen together, except when they want to fu...except during the mating season."

"But I thought there was only one, you know, the legendary creature from myth that no one ever sees." she whined.

"Sorry miss, there are quite a few, even hundreds, this is a big swamp." Chada laughed.

One of the crew spoke, a single word, whispered.

Chada turned around and glared at him.

"What is it? What did he say?"

Chada forced a smile over his scowl. "It's nothing really, just a legend...no not exactly that, more an exaggeration, really."

"Tell me." The princess said, sieving through Chada's emotions, looking for a useful one. She found pride, and rode it like a wild horse across his good sense.

"There is a tale about a gagrog, a big one. Probably three times the size of the one down there. I've never seen it, but many say they have. It lives in a certain pool at the centre of the swamp. That's the one they call 'hadagrogida' which translates as 'eater of boats'. They say this one is the father of all, and that's where the name gagrog comes from."

"Take me there, take me there now." Oleana-tarli demanded in her best royal voice. She then took up position in the bow, an animated figurehead, and its hair wafting on the slight breeze.

Chada turned to his crew and sighed with acceptance. "Ready with the oars boys, let's take the lady to her beast." Under his breath he muttered, "not to say we'll be bringing her back, right royal pain in the ar...backside."

Seventeen

"'Manoeuvres', what exactly are they anyway?" Shemaz grumbled.

"Are you still going on about that?" K'treema answered testily.

"I just what to know what they are and why did the entire bloody garrison of Esh decide to manoeuvre now, just when we need them?"

"They have to practice Maz, to keep in readiness for war, especially this close to Oq."

"Oq's days away, weeks even, unless you've got a big horse. And why can't they manoeuvre nearer to Esh?"

"According to the soldier they left behind, they were practising hill warfare, and so had to go to Dun Sa peaks. Which are only a one day ride from Esh, so we should soon find them." K'treema explained patiently.

"Why do they need hill practice, there aren't any real hills for miles?"

"Yes, but there are plenty of hills in Iamunaya."

Shemaz was thoughtful for a few seconds, then her face lit up, "Ah! I see." And with this she was satisfied for a while.

"Manoeuvres." She said, a while later.

"Don't start that again." K'treema scolded with a sigh.

"I wasn't," Shemaz protested loudly, "I was just saying manoeuvres, its a nice word isn't it, sort of rolls off the tongue? Manoeuvres."

K'treema raised her eyebrows but said nothing.

"So how's your neck?" Shemaz said into the silence.

Glad of a change of subject, K'treema brightened. "It isn't so sore now, since we put on some of that herbal stuff. Whiffs a bit though, very similar to the old pedlar we bought it off."

"That'll be the goose fat, they always start with that, easy to get hold of I suppose. But you're right; mine's eased off a lot. Wonder what it was though, I thought it was the cord on the necklace, but it only started the other day, after we dealt with those slinks the night before," Shemaz mused.

"I wondered that too, the redness was underneath the necklaces and nowhere else, almost like a burn, as though the string had rubbed against our skin. Perhaps its because we are moving more, making them swing around."

"We haven't moved any more than usual, and we did buy them right at the beginning of our Journey. Why didn't they chaff then?"

K'treema lifted her necklace and rubbed underneath it, the warmer part that had touched her skin. She concentrated on the edge as she walked, feeling for roughness or unevenness that would explain the sore neck.

A slight tingle ran through her fingertips, an unfamiliar yet comforting flick of power, just like when she gathered her magic. She took a sharp breath, eyes widening, she stumbled jarringly as the thought hit. "Magic, it feels like magic."

Shemaz stopped. "What, what does? The necklace?" She too lifted her own necklace and carefully examined it. "How did that get in there? You don't suppose it leaked in from our bodies do you?"

"No, it wouldn't have burned us, not our own power. No, it was put there, put there by the only person we know who could have done it."

"Dhomag."

"Right, and why did he do that then?"

"Because he thinks our magic is puny, so he gave us a little help." Shemaz speculated.

"Of course, that's why we were able to see off the slinks and not feel tired, the magic came from the necklaces, not us."

K'treema and Shemaz turned to face each other. Their eyes met and widened, their mouths twisted in disgust. Together they chorused, "Ugh, mage magic!" And pulled the coral jewellery off, dropping them onto the sandy trail.

The two wizards stood around the offending articles looking down at them. "What now?" Shemaz asked.

"Well, we have to find the soldiers to warn them, and we can't leave mage magic just lying around, so we'll have to take them."

"We'll have to put them in our packs, wrap them in something. Come on." Shemaz bent down and lifted her necklace as though it were a dead snake. Carefully, she removed a foot stocking from her pack and fed the jewellery right down into the toe. K'treema did the same; wrapping hers in a woollen scarf her mother had insisted she take. "This is silly, we've been wearing them for days."

"Yes, and look what they've done to our necks. Who knows what they could have done if we'd left them on. I'm going to make him take the magic out when I see him again, mage or no mage," Shemaz scowled.

"How do you know we will? He might just wander off somewhere," K'treema said, shouldering her pack and setting off.

"Oh, he'll show up again. After all, he can find us, or our back packs at least."

The wizards were ambushed just as they came in sight of the Dun Sa peaks. The collection of low hills spread across the horizon like an uneven green cloth. Two soldiers leapt out from behind a collection of bushes, swords in hand. To her consternation, K'treema's hand flew up to her neck, feeling for the now missing necklace, she felt vulnerable without its promised extra kick of power.

Shemaz wasn't so easily shocked, and challenged the men. "What are you doing leaping out on people like that? You could have startled us to death."

"Sorry, wise ones," the older of the two said. "We thought you were the other side come up to catch us from behind."

"What, Iamunayans here already?"

"Iamunayans? No wise one, just our men, you know, from the other team," he laughed, glancing at the younger man, "You won't find any of those bog-drinkers around here."

"Unless you take us to your commander straight away I wouldn't be so sure," Shemaz said calmly, fixing the man with her gaze.

Both soldiers suddenly stopped smiling. "Are you jesting, Wise one?" The younger one asked, hopping from foot to foot.

"No, not at all, so let's get a move on before we are all drinking bog water."

The commanding officer was eventually found atop a flattened hill, surrounded by men who were all on their stomachs. At the bottom of the hill other men worked slowly upwards in a similar fashion.

"What are they doing?" K'treema asked.

"Manoeuvres miss."

Shemaz looked at K'treema and smiled, but was silenced by a glare from her tall friend.

After the younger soldier had been and explained, they were soon sat under a spreading tree accepting the captain's hospitality. Over cups of spiced water and fresh army bread, which was a hollow loaf filled with a wide range of finely chopped meat and vegetables, the two wizards explained the entire situation to captain Saratil of the Emperor's Borderers (Esh Run.)

Captain Saratil was a man of few words, most of them spoken loudly and immediately acted upon by one or more men. He was exactly how anyone would picture an active soldier, tall, wide shouldered, firm looking, with a grim visage and a jet-black moustache. Only the obligatory scar was missing, at least on the parts they could see.

Once the story was told, Saratil ran off a full list of orders and the entire hillside of soldiers was suddenly on the move. Less than a dozen minutes later, two very impressed wizards were mounted on pack horses and were heading back towards Esh, in the company of the captain and several other handsome officers. As they veered off, K'treema looked back, and was surprised to see the actual amount of men that had emerged from the hills. There were quite a few, but didn't in any way look like an army. Still, she thought, an Empire soldier was worth ten of the king's, so perhaps there would be enough.

The column rode through the night, arriving on the plains of Esh just after sunrise. A lone soldier, who came galloping out of the east gate at breakneck speed, greeted them. When he had pulled to a stop in a shower of soil and sod, he gasped out, "Bog drinkers sir, sorry sir, Iamunayans sir, approaching the west gate, hundreds sir, quick sir, can't shut the gates sir, never been closed for years sir."

With his usual calm and efficient manner, the captain issued his orders. The men were split into three groups, two would ride around Esh and a smaller one would go through the middle, hoping to catch the enemy in a pincer movement. The soldiers moved off at a gallop, keen to drive away the invaders.

K'treema and Shemaz were to accompany the captain into Esh, but he made it quite clear that as wizards their aid would be expected. They were to go in behind the first line of soldiers and do what they could. The two wizards looked at each other, then at their backpacks, but neither spoke.

The east gate soon stood open before them, and they quickly passed beneath the walls of the old town. As they rode through, crafts people were working on the gates, trying to free the bound hinges. It had been many years since the town had needed to close the gates; life under the emperor was mostly peaceful.

Everywhere around the town was a bustle of activity; people unused to such threats were rushing around haphazardly, doing the things they thought ought to be done when an army approached. Many of the towns folks stopped and cheered as the band rode by, some calling out encouragement and slurs on the enemy.

K'treema and Shemaz sat grimly atop their mounts, both refusing to think about the power in the packs, power they may shortly need.

Despite the milling crowds, the group were soon at the west gate. The captain ordered his men to dismount and form a half circle around the open entrance. Here too, crafts people worked on the hinges, pouring in oil and rocking the great wooden structures back and forth. Each time they swung, a loud creaking filled the air, but each time the gate moved a little further.

Looking through the gates, the wizards were shocked to see the enemy approaching, some mounted to either side, the rest on foot. They were terribly close, too close for the gates to be closed in time, though not a single person stopped trying.

K'treema looked across to Shemaz, who with a shrug was removing her pack. "We are going to need it 'Tree, we can't let these people suffer if we can help." she pulled out her stocking and fished around inside.

K'treema took a deep breath, then swearing a curse on Dhomag, she too pulled out the necklace and fastened it around her neck. Neither of them were sure they needed to be worn, but they couldn't risk it not working.

The Iamunayans were closer now, their war cries growing louder as they came on. The gates swung again, this time stopping a cart width apart. But the invaders were too close for another try, so the crafts people leaned against them, hoping to at least channel the enemy into a smaller space. The soldiers moved up, closing the semi circle tighter around the gate.

Then the first of the invaders were upon them, battering into the wood with a sound like horses on a wooden bridge. The gates moved slightly, then more, as the weight of the invaders pressed against it.

Screams sounded, as the enemy were pierced with arrows from the ring of men. And still the gates moved, slowly but inexorably open. From their horses, K'treema and Shemaz could see the struggle clearly, and after a rushed consultation, they called up their powers.

In her heart, K'treema could feel the mage magic sitting on her own, like a huge dam, holding back immense power. But the dam was black in her mind, seething and organic, draining strength from her surroundings like blood from a child. She put the picture out of her mind, and concentrated on making a wedge of power, not a fist, but an open hand, to jab between the gates.

Shemaz felt the mage power too, and remembered all the stories she had been told, about mages scouring the ground so that nothing grew, how they bled the world of goodness until there was nothing left. But surely this amount of power wouldn't hurt? She was hardly casting huge soul burning blasts of fire. So she too concentrated, and hoped no one would notice the boost she was getting.

A whirlwind sprang into life between the soldiers and the gates; the biggest Shemaz had ever managed. The soldiers stopped shooting as their arrows were snatched up by the wind. They stood calm and still, all having seen the wizards on their Journeys. The wind approached the gates, and began to push and batter against it. The invaders caught in the wind were blinded by the dust and struck by the whirling arrows. The crafts folk to either side pulled back, but were too in awe of the magic to move away.

The gates creaked, the whirlwind howled faster and faster as Shemaz tapped the well of mage energy. The enemy soldiers nearest the wind tried to pull back, but were crushed by those moving in from behind. A shimmering appeared in the air just above ground level as K'treema too drew on the mage power from her necklace. A hand was shaped from the air. It hung still for a second, then smashed through the gap as K'treema released it, her body shaking with joy.

Full-grown men were suddenly propelled backwards as the power struck them. Feet left drag marks in the ground as they were pushed away from the gates. The war cries died as screams took their place. The whirlwind pushed the groaning timbers on reluctant hinges, and slowly the gates began to close.

But the invaders were too tightly packed to dislodge so

easily, and the gates soon caught again. K'treema gathered up more power, and was surprised to find it somewhat depleted. Still, she had not yet used her own inner strength, and there was enough mage magic for another strike.

The hand formed again. This time the invaders recognised it and began to scramble out of the way, calling out to those behind to move. Too late, the hand shot forwards, scattering bodies like stands of corn. The whirlwind whined once more and the gates slammed closed, trapping enemy limbs between and underneath in a cacophony of screams, creaks and cracking bones.

K'treema and Shemaz turned away from the carnage, removing the necklaces and stowing them back in their packs. Neither felt the tiredness of magic use, but both felt keenly the mixed emotions of exhilaration and the taint of using mage magic.

Town's folk dashed forwards and swung the bolts, sealing the invaders out, just as the two columns of empire soldiers arrived. The horsemen drove towards the gate, catching the king's men in disarray. The attack on Esh faltered and died as the invaders grouped themselves into a rough circle and retreated back towards the border. Unwilling to commit to a large battle at this point, the captain recalled his men. They entered the town, through the east gate, to a clamorous welcome. The west gates were so thoroughly closed it took the crafts people almost four days to unseal them.

Eighteen

A small marsh craft drifted, apparently empty, on the edge of a wide-open pool. This pool looked exactly like any other pool in the swamp, but was several times bigger. It lay in the middle of a series of crescent moon shaped islands, a maze of dead ends and false exits. Marshwater Chada had successfully navigated his way to the middle though, with a little encouragement from Oleana-tarli. All they had to do now was wait, the princess, the guide and his two crew either crouched or sprawled out across the deck.

All was quiet, discounting the frogs calling, the birds screeching, and the deep, booming vibration Chada said was the hadagrogida, calling to his mate. Oleana-tarli listened with one ear against the wood of the hull. The deepest sound she had ever heard rumbled into her brain, deeper than the message drums, deeper than thunder. And it was getting louder, closer.

Chada's eyes widened impossibly as he realised what was happening. "Grab onto something, quick. She won't sink, not this boat, not my baby." This last seemed to be more a prayer than a statement. He braced himself against the hull, gripping the wooden rail with white knuckles. The princess did the same, gripping the wood until her hands hurt, then gripping tighter.

The marsh fell silent, the animals stilled and the booming stopped. At first, they all thought the creature had gone, but Oleana-tarli suddenly noticed the trees begin to shrink, as though the islands were being pulled under the water.

Except it wasn't the trees shrinking, it was the boat rising, so slowly and smoothly that it was difficult to tell they were moving. Further they went, until they were convinced that a giant bubble of marsh gas had lifted the boat. For surely no creature was this tall, yet could hide in such shallow water.

The boat tilted, end on to the water, leaving Oleana-tarli swinging by her hands. Chada and the crew, having more experience, had braced their feet as well, and were now standing on wooden supports that were formally vertical struts. A flask of wine slid along the deck, tangled in loose rope, then smashed into the stern, showering one of the crew with pottery and wine he could never afford.

Again the boat tipped, forwards now, causing the princess to flip a half circle, cracking her feet into the hull just beside Chada's face. Bottle fragments and other

unsecured items slithered the length of the deck. An oar
caught one of the crew on his shoulder, his grip loosened,
and momentarily he was in danger of falling.

The boat righted again, steadied for a moment, and
began to fall. It picked up speed, hitting the water with
a slapping, cracking sound. Oleana-tarli heard a sob of
anguish from Chada before being dragged under the
surface by the submerging rail.

The wooden vessel bobbed back up, and then dipped
again. Quickly, she took a breath, then as the boat went
under for a second time, she kicked away, pushing at
the rail with her feet to get a good start. Using the waves
produced by the boat, she swam gracefully to a muddy
bank and dragged herself onto it. She tried to stand, but
fell backwards as she turned to survey the damage, landing
with a splat, burying herself ears deep in dark mud.

When she was finally able to sit upright Chada's baby
was still making waves. Underneath the rail, a darker
shade than the water, a vast shape moved a cavernous
mouth slowly up and down. The boat was actually sitting
on the hadagrogida's back, resting edge on at the mercy of
the beast. Oleana-tarli saw movement on the boat, Chada's
head appeared, disappeared, reappeared further along.
He began to shout orders, but ears filled with mud weren't
able to catch what he was saying.

All went quiet on board. Then, slowly, the oars began to
protrude from the back. A few minutes went by, a rocking
motion started, swaying the vessel side to side. At first the
princess thought the gagrog was getting serious, meaning
to smash the boat and live up to its name. When the boat
finally rolled over, the oars were thrust into the water, and
the crew began to row for all they were worth.

The gagrog didn't notice for a good few oar strokes,
then rose slowly behind the boat, opening its mouth and
slowing the vessel by taking in massive amounts of water,
dragging it backwards.

Oleana-tarli was about to shout encouragement when
she suddenly realised the boat was going without her.
"Hey Chada," she shouted in her best I'm-not-a-princess

voice, "get back here and get me out of this mud!"

Chada turned, waved, a wide smile on his face, and then turned back to the task of saving his boat.

"Chada!" she screeched, in her best princess voice, "Get back here at once, or the king shall hear of this!" She stamped her foot, a gesture made completely ineffective by the calf deep mud she was standing in.

When even this, her best royal command didn't work, the princess dived into the water and began to swim after him. She'd show him how to behave in the presence of royalty, she'd have him naked and covered in honey-worms and thrown into the hen house before he could shout mercy. With practised strokes that had won her the admiration of many a suitor, she surfaced and stroked off after the boat. Gagrog or no gagrog, she would teach this man a lesson.

Oleana-tarli stopped swimming, trod water for a few moments. What was she doing, she thought, she had a gagrog, she didn't need a puny wooden boat. Now, how do I call a gagrog? She realised it was a bit late to be thinking this, but after all she didn't have much choice. So she set off again, wide strokes, chin up, mud trailing behind her.

Chada and his crew pulled the oars with all their hearts, dragging them faster than they had ever done before. Chada was working to save his boat, the crew to stay alive, but the result was the same. A gagrog no matter how big still cannot swallow a whole marsh of water. Inevitably, the water had to stabilize, leaving the crew to row effectively, driving the craft back the way they had come.

The distance between creature and boat increased as they settled into a steady rhythm. The gagrog seemed to have lost interest now they weren't directly above it. Chada left the crew to row, and leaned out of the stern. "Ah! Beat you, you bag of swamp gas, you over grown water skin, you big gobbed, useless fu...bas...shit head." And he roared with laughter. Quickly, he scanned the area for signs of his passenger, not finding her on the mud bank, or anywhere else, he shrugged his shoulders and turned back to the safe navigation of his baby back home.

Oleana-tarli watched him go, treading water, wiping the mud from her face and ears. The gagrog rose to the surface, its broad back like a leather boat. It turned, spinning in the water like a swivel bridge opening. When finally it was facing her, it began to move towards her, its mouth opening wider as it came on.

"No, not me you fool, I'm your new mistress!" She shouted. The gagrog didn't slow. Nervously, she took a few strokes, moving to the creature's right, out of its direct path. The hadagrogida turned also, its mouth wider still. In panic now, Oleana-tarli launched herself through the water, grabbing wide armfuls of swamp water and pushing them behind her. The beast, although seemingly in no hurry, kept up without any visible effort.

Although an accomplished swimmer, her tutors had often told her so, she was beginning to tire. Her arms became heavier in the water, her breath deeper and more laboured, and still hadagrogida came on. Every time she moved, it too changed course. The only hope she had was to get to an island and try to out run it. Looking frantically about, she was dismayed to see all the islands too far away to make before the creature could reach her. She set off nevertheless; she wasn't going to let this bog swiller taste rich food, not without a good fight. She pulled to one side, waited for the creature to turn, then quickly changed direction and went the other way. She was well away from the gagrog by the time it had turned, but was still no closer to the relative safety of the islands. A thought hit her. When she had turned, the gagrog hadn't been able to keep up. She tried again, and sure enough, it was only able to rotate at a fraction of its swimming speed.

Hastily, Oleana-tarli chose an island, the largest and nearest, then began to turn the gagrog until it faced away from it. With a sudden sprint, she changed direction; swimming towards the gagrog, swimming down the side it was turning away from. With her last strength, she swam for her life, whilst the creature tried to find her.

Its mouth opened as she swam, water rushing in, but

she was too far away to be affected. Painfully slowly the island neared, and suddenly she felt her feet kick into the soft mud of the lakebed. A few more strokes and she was only waist deep in the water.

She risked a look back, and looked straight into the gaping mouth of the eater of boats. Half walking, half swimming, she struggled the last few steps, her breath gasping in damp air and drops of swamp water. The mud squelched between her toes as she fought for the bank. A blast of warm air blew around her body as the gagrog closed. At last her feet left the water and she was able to run, panic alone giving her the energy to move. Oleana-tarli slapped and sank ankle deep up the bank, kicking mud and long worm like creatures in all directions. The top of the bank was lined with many-rooted trees, each sending three or four slim trunks into the humid air. She grabbed at them and pulled herself up, slipping between the trunks, pressing on a good way from the water. When all sight of the brown creature was gone she stopped, gripped at a trunk and rested her head in her arms. She took deep breaths, steadying her thumping heart.

A cracking of branches caused her head to shoot up, her breathing to stop. Had she saved herself from the gagrog to be stalked by some swamp cat? The trees creaked in the distance, snapped, and were crushed under what sounded like a massive weight. Oleana-tarli mentally slapped herself. Of course it could move on land, how else was she going to get it to the battlefield?

Cursing herself for an undeserving idiot, she set off again, silently moving in a diagonal direction back to the water. She soon came in sight of the creature. Her first glance of its true size made her stare in awe. It was easily twice as long as Chada's boat, as tall as two men, and wider than the main gate of the palace. Its head alone could have contained the royal carriage, and its legs were thicker than even the thickest columns in the coronation room.

But it was brown, plain brown all over, with skin like old leather. And not a single horn or mighty tooth to be seen. Oleana-tarli started as she realised the gagrog was looking back, studying her with its fist-sized eye.

Slowly, moving as the gagrog did, she approached the beast closer, thinking calm thoughts and speaking quiet, unthreatening words. With no more energy left to run, and still convinced the vision was right, she approached the hadagrogida, holding out her hands to show she meant no harm. The gagrog didn't move, just stood like a giant lumpy bag, its legs sunk deeply into the soft soil of the island.

Perhaps, the princess thought, now it can see me it knows who I am. Perhaps it too had a vision. Who knew what went on in the mind of the biggest animal she had ever seen.

She was close enough to touch it now. Her fingertips outstretched; she gently let them brush against the gagrog's hide. It was warm, warmer than she was, and felt like the sponges the merchants claimed came from the sea. The massive head swung around to keep its eye facing her, the deep orb looked colourless in the patch of sunlight it had created. The pupil showed only darkness, as though she looked along a tunnel.

Well, she thought, step one completed, all she needed now was a set of horns, some really big teeth, a way to guide it, and then all she had to do was move it to a battlefield she didn't know across half a continent. She shrugged. This needs work, and I do my best work whilst I'm naked.

Quickly she slipped out of her mud caked clothes, and stood bare in front of the gagrog. The mud felt slippery and cool against her skin, and really quite nice. She spent a little time on the muddy bank, rolling in it and covering herself all over.

The gagrog backed into the water until only its head showed, and watched with great interest.

Nineteen

In a barn somewhere near the west gate of Esh, two figures slept in each other's arms like new borns. The bleating of a goat disturbed the alcohol inspired dreams of the men. For a moment or two, reality and dreams overlapped, evoking strange visions of thundering herds of cloven-hoofed monsters with beer barrel eyes.

Dhomag sat upright, awoken by a strange shiver. His head spun as though someone had just whipped it like a child's toy. Memories seeped back, his name, where he was, who the strange man beside him was. There didn't appear to be too much to remember, but this didn't overly worry him.

A certain point was reached in his memories of himself. And the magic rose up within him. Something was wrong it said, there was some form of attack it didn't recognise. It flared anyway, igniting the straw, rolling the prone body away with the blast. The goat bleated in distress, a ball of energy shot from Dhomag's finger, removed the goat's left horn just above its head and burned a neat hole in a support beam.

The flames spread, travelling along his comrade's legs, causing the man to roll over screaming and shouting. Concentrating, Dhomag enveloped himself in a blue glow, and burned away the residue of alcohol and over indulgence. Then calmly he extinguished the flames with a pass of his hand.

His friend Talco continued to bat at himself for a while longer, then stopped, looked at Dhomag through pitifully red eyes, and groaned loudly. "Oh, my head, oh my back, oh my legs. What a nightmare, I thought I was on fire." He slumped back into the straw, clamping his hands over his eyes.

"Well, shall we get breakfast? I could eat a goat," Dhomag asked brightly.

"Breakfast? How can you eat? You drank twice as much as me, and I can put it away. No, you want it, go, but don't disturb me until that drum stops playing."

Dhomag grinned to himself, waving his hands over Talco Farm.

His comrade went still as his exposed skin flushed a deep pink. The heat quickly subsided, and Falco moved his hand, just enough to look out with one eye. "It's stopped then, good." He opened his other eye. "And someone's put out that bright light."

A smile crept across his face. "Well, it seems I didn't have as much as I thought. Did you mention breakfast? Let's go."

At that moment the door swung open, and a very angry looking man with a large pitchfork entered. He glared at the goat, the fire damaged straw, and at the two men. He advanced, the bright tangs aimed straight at Dhomag.

Dhomag smiled, a wide toothy grin filled with so much warmth the straw almost re-ignited. "Good morning good sir, we were just coming to look for you."

"You were?" the man replied, a puzzled expression on his face. The pitchfork was raised slowly until it pointed to the ceiling.

"Yes, we had a very comfortable night in your barn, and it's only proper that we offer some payment. No, we insist," Dhomag insisted before the poor farmer could even speak, never mind decline the offer. Dhomag held out a large coin, engraved with a running horse. "Ah, a full stallion should do it."

Falco almost choked, and the farmer's eyes went wide with disbelief. This coin was worth half a season's income to a poor farmer. The man grabbed it before the bargain could be withdrawn, biting the coin, and then scratching it with a grubby thumbnail. Satisfied, the farmer beamed, stuffed the coin in a handy pocket, and escorted his guests out into the street.

It was a bright morning, with a hint of cloud. Dhomag stretched, taking in a deep breath and feeling better than he had in a lifetime. As the pair set off, Dhomag felt a familiar warmth run through his mind. Looking around, he saw two figures walking away from him.

A simple thought stopped the women and turned them around. Eyes met, mage and wizard, then wizard and mage.

"Dhomag?" Shemaz called, "what are you doing here?"

"Shouldn't you be guarding the border?" K'treema added.

"What for, there aren't any more soldiers, my friend Talco here has been showing me around." Dhomag turned and indicated the empty space next to him. He looked around, but there was no sign of his new friend. A quick scan of the crowd showed him to be nowhere around. The mage shrugged, "Oh, I think he's a little shy around women, especially such beautiful ones as you two."

K'treema and Shemaz smiled, but didn't blush. This time, his charm lasted only moments before they were back to business. Slowly, but very firmly, the two wizards stepped either side of the mage and led him back to the west gate. Thick timbers had been used to seal the gate closed, but only after they had been repaired, and could now be swung in either direction on the finely balanced hinges. All around the gate, in every available flat area, the enemy dead had been laid out, stripped of weapons and valuables, then covered with thin sheets.

K'treema pointed to a large pile of armour, decorated with the stylised bird. "Do you remember that emblem?"

Dhomag shifted uncomfortably, and answered, "Yes, of course, they are the king's men, the same as the ones I dealt with in the wilds."

"That's right, and do you know where they came from?"

"Across the border?" Dhomag suggested.

"Correct. And who was guarding the border?"

Sighing, Dhomag turned to face K'treema, looking straight into her eyes. "K'treema, it's a long border, I am only one man, I can't be everywhere at once."

"Yes, it's true, I'm sorry, even you can't do that," K'treema said, her voice soft and breathy. Her heart was beating like a blacksmith's anvil on shoeing day. Dhomag's face was close now; his sweet breath caressed her face as gentle as a petal. Nearer he came, his body heat almost palpable. Warmth spread from her stomach and over her body, intensifying around her nipples and between her legs. Her lips parted ready to receive his.

"But you weren't on the border, not any of it. You were in here, doing what?" Shemaz demanded, spinning him around to face her. K'treema almost fell over with the sudden removal.

Dhomag's eyes met those of Shemaz. "I'm only human, I need to eat and drink too, perhaps not as often, but it's still true."

"Oh, well, of course, you can't make yourself ill over this, you'd be no good to us then," Shemaz sighed, her eyes growing a little moist at the corners.

She tried unsuccessfully to fight the rising heat in her face as Dhomag moved close. A feeling of intense excitement filled her, as well as a sense of danger. Both feelings produced a need in her, and she knew, at that moment, that if Dhomag had suggested they make love, she would have grabbed his arm and ran with him to the nearest bed.

"So why do you smell of beer and goats, and why is there straw in your hair, and what the sheep's arse is that on your back?" K'treema, now recovered, pulled him away from Shemaz and glared at him, trying her utmost to remain calm. Shemaz swayed back and forth before recovering her composition.

He had mostly forgotten his sword, but was pleased now to remember it. Taking a few steps back, he reached over his shoulder and grabbed hold of the hilt. "This." He pulled, "This!" He pulled harder, "this is my new weapon, especially picked for me by my friend Talco." Finally the sword scraped free of the sheath. The blade was easily as long as Shemaz, notched, but basically sound, if not exactly sharp. The quillons sprouted from the hilt and curled out then back, forming a pair of swans necks. The handgrip itself was long enough for four hands to hold, wrapped in blue dyed leather and obviously hardly used. Finished with a ball pommel carved into the shape of some kind of fruit, the whole weapon was longer than Dhomag was tall, forcing him to wear it diagonally across his back.

The sword glinted in the sun as Dhomag arced it back and forth. It became fairly clear almost immediately that Dhomag should concentrate on magic, as his swordsmanship left a lot to be desired. Quickly the wizards backed away from the web of death, as Dhomag, like so many men with a weapon in their hands, deluded himself to be some kind of master.

"What do you think ladies?" Dhomag asked, a look of pure pleasure on his face.

"Yes, very nice, now could you put it away, you're lethal with that thing," K'treema called.

"Do you really think so? You know, Talco said it was the perfect weapon for me. I wonder where he's gone?" Reluctantly, Dhomag removed the sheath and returned the sword to it, putting it back in its original place.

"Who is this man? This Talco, doesn't sound like a local," Shemaz asked suspiciously.

"He's not, I met him out there, near the border, he was hiding behind a rock."

K'treema and Shemaz glanced at each other, eyes wide, then back at Dhomag. "You met him near the border..."

"Hiding behind a rock..."

"And you led him back here?"

"Are you mad, what if he's a spy?"

Dhomag looked at his feet, "Well he seemed nice enough."

The two wizards looked at each other, exchanged a message with facial expressions, then took hold of Dhomag and led him away from the gate. When they had found a quiet corner under the shade of the town walls, they sat down on a row of barrels. K'treema looked at Dhomag, then quickly turned away, "Dhomag, we know you are a mage, and probably the most powerful man in the empire, but what about other people, don't you care what happens to them? What if this man had led the king's men in here at night? The whole town could have been wiped out. You should be protecting these people, not putting them in danger."

Dhomag was quiet for a few moments. His hands came up and he rubbed his face. "I'd like to help, really, but my mind is empty. The only thing I really remember from before is my oath to kill the emperor. I don't know where the magic came from; I do know I didn't have it before. I know how to use it though; I suppose that comes with it. I know where it comes from and where it goes, and how to make it do those things. But feelings are a blur. There was somebody, a person I cared for, but they… she… is long gone. It's all just so confusing, and it hurts when I try to remember. So I don't. The way I am, or the way I'm being, covers up the pain."

Dhomag looked at K'treema, then at Shemaz. "Don't you see? I can't be caring for others when it takes all my energy to care for me. Perhaps later, when things are more settled, perhaps when things… memories… return, then I'll be fine. Now, there's just my oath, and I intend to fulfil it."

"Dhomag, can't you understand? The emperor that did those terrible things to you is long dead; the emperor is good, as was his father and grandfather. The empire has never been as prosperous, as settled, as at peace than it is now. We have laws we have schools. Look at us, at one time we would have been rounded up and held as slaves in the emperor's dungeons. Now we walk free, are respected by the community. You can't blame this emperor for the crimes of a thousand years ago."

The mage thought long and hard in silence, the shadows visibly moved by the time he spoke. "I suppose you're right, revenge on the wrong person is no revenge at all. But what else do I have? Memories are pain, I have no place in this world, no trade or family, no ties at all."

Shemaz rested her hand on his shoulder, "You have us, we can be your family, and I'm sure a man of your talents could soon find himself in demand."

"I'll think about it, but to be honest, I don't see you as sisters at all, no not at all." He couldn't suppress a smile.

"So, what about this invasion, if that's what it is." K'treema said loudly, feeling a change of subject was called for here.

Shemaz stood, "yes, we're needed here, it would be a great help if you could stand with us."

"I need to think, my head is spinning. Talco tells me one thing and you say something different."

"But he's a spy, or at least one of the king's men, you can't believe anything he says." Shemaz protested. "You need to look at the bigger picture."

"I need to think, I'm going home for a while."

"But you said you don't have a home."

"Well, back to the desert, to the rocks I came out of. I can rest there, see what comes into my head." He stood, kissed them both on the cheek. He walked away, fading as if he entered a fog.

The two wizards were so amazed they forgot to tell him to remove the magic from their necklaces.

Twenty

It was cold that night; Oleana-tarli was forced to dress for the first time in three days. Fortunately, she had rinsed her clothes and dried them as best she could in the damp atmosphere. Those days had been spent trying to figure out the gagrog. At no time had it showed any aggression towards her since she had drawn it from the water, but neither did it allow her to mount it or examine it closer. She was permitted to touch it, indeed it seemed to like being stroked, emitting an almost inaudible rumble that caused the water to dance.

But nothing else could she make it do. Yet all the time it watched her, studied her, as though it waited for her to reveal something about herself.

She curled up in the pile of flattened leaves she was using for a bed. Every night she had gone over her vision, every night the same result; a vivid picture of what she perceived as truth, but not a single clue as to how she arrived there.

Oleana-tarli was tired; she hadn't slept well at all. Used as she was to a soft mattress and a gentle cooling breeze, surrounded by armed guards, each ready to die for her. Now, all she had was the semi-comforting presence of the gagrog and a pile of damp, probably infested leaves. She sighed, settled herself as best she could, and determined to sleep.

Dreams ran through her head, of pursuit by a hoard of beheaded guards, of something dark searching for her, of tall men with enormous erections demanding she satisfy them all. The princess awoke with a spasm of muscles and sat quickly upright. The dawn was just rising, casting a grey light across the brown swamp. In the water, only the top of its long head showing, the gagrog watched. A procession of long, many legged insects was walking over her ankle, some scattered by her sudden movement. Squealing with disgust, she leapt up and brushed herself down, starting at her feet and moving up to the top of her head, where she shook her hair until she was dizzy.

Oleana-tarli eyed the gagrog, "today, you and I are going to sort out who's in charge around here." She pointed, assumed the most imperious stance she could manage, "then we're going to take a ride. We're going to find that guide and his precious boat, and trample it to tooth picks." Then, she thought, I'm going to take a bath, eat cooked food, drink fine wine, and have abandoned, public sex with the first man who comes up to my standards. In that order.

Pulling herself together, the princess tried her best to appear regal, if not in dress, then in stance and stature. She realised her lovely hair was a mess, her clothes had virtually disappeared under a layer of mud, and her fine baby skin was covered with grime, but she wasn't going to let that ruin her day. After all, only the gagrog was watching, it didn't really matter.

Trying to remember all she had been taught, Oleana-tarli stood before the gagrog. The beast had risen a good distance from the water as she prepared herself, as if it knew she was about to make her move. Tutors and lessons slipped across her mind, male tutors touching her legs and being dragged away. Female teachers walking out in disgust, slammed doors, the shouting of 'guard!' lectures from the king on duty and responsibility.

And finally, there was miss Milily, a woman of middle age, of unremarkable appearance, of infinite patience and the guile of a whole colony of foxes. It was she who finally settled her down to study, who taught her to read and write and sew and think. How to use a library and the people around her. How to be a princess with the maximum freedom for the minimum price. Oleana-tarli smiled fondly, a whole head full of warm images.

The gagrog sunk slowly in the water, a glassy look in its wide eyes.

Of course, Milily had left, when Oleana-tarli was too old for tutors. A sadder day there had never been, tears all around, hugs and promises to write, to visit. One of the worst days of her life so far, she cried herself to sleep that night. Oleana-tarli wiped away a little moisture in the corner of her eye, and sighed.

The gagrog let out a huffing breath, blinking rapidly in the brightening morning.

So all she needed do now was remember some of those things. She realised her mood could affect others, except her father, who was just as good at it. Briefly, she wondered if an animal could be similarly influenced. Did beasts have enough of a brain to be persuaded? As a child, she'd had a bird that could talk, but she wasn't sure if it understood what it was saying. Perhaps all animals were the same, reacting to certain events, rather than thinking for themselves. With one hand to her face, she stood for several minutes frantically trying to bring up every memory of every animal she had ever encountered.

The gagrog rose a distance from the water until its shoulders appeared. It stood very still for a while, looking into the distance, its eyebrow ridges furrowed.

Nothing helped; no animal she had ever met had matched in any way the size and strangeness of the gagrog. She would have to try something else.

It wasn't fair, why did she have to be born a princess? If she'd been an ordinary girl she would have been in that water now, wrestling the thing into submission. She fumed at life's unfairness, at all the things people had done to her to deprive her of being queen.

A waft of warm air blew across her face. Absently she looked down, to see the water around the gagrog steaming slightly. Her mouth fell open. Carefully she reached out a foot and dipped a toe into the murky water. Around the gagrog it was hot, further away the water was barely warm.

When she looked again the water had stopped steaming, and the gagrog was watching her with a calm expression. Puzzled, Oleana-tarli tried to remember what had been on her mind when she first noticed the creature's reaction. Angry, she thought, I was angry. Angry with all the injustice. She stamped her food with a loud splash into the waters edge, stoking her wrath.

The gagrog rose to its feet, the water that ran off as it stood emitting drifts of vapour. All around it, the other swamp creatures scooted off as the water temperature increased. Its skin was pink now, not the usual dull brown. Its hide had also tightened, shrunk in some way, so that the princess could make out a few muscles and the beginnings of a beast more like the one in her vision.

She jumped in the air, screamed in victory, and landed with a loud splat on the muddy bank. "Well well, at last we see your true colours, and it's so early in the morning, let's see what else we can do." Oleana-tarli looked straight into the eye of the beast, an eye now longer, narrower, and with a spark of fire in the centre. Both creatures now understood the situation, and both realised one was no good without the other.

"Let's get started then," Oleana-tarli said, "and I'm sick of this water, so let's get out of it and get down to some serious fun."

She formed an image in her mind of dry land. She yearned for it and wished for it with all her heart. The gagrog pulled its massive bulk from the water and walked onto the island, flattening bushes and reeds deep into the mud. Following in its trail, the princess kept her thoughts concentrated until they came across a wide space on the highest point on the isle. It wasn't open space, but it was dry and away from all that mud. Moving its weight with impressive speed, the gagrog trampled around until every bush and stunted tree was flat. So good a job did it do, the pair now stood in a wide depression.

In the middle of the clearing, the gagrog and the princess faced each other. With a deep breath, Oleana-tarli relaxed, forming the image in her mind of the vision, of the mighty gagrog trampling and gouging its way through the helpless bodies of the empire soldiers.

Before her, its skin flushing pink then darkening to red, the gagrog steamed until it was dry, then burned. Thin peels of skin began to flake off and ignite, rising into the air like paper from a bonfire. The princess was dumbstruck, but held the image, afraid to let go now that she had finally found it.

The huge animal began to change. The skin, now cherry red, shrank, the eyes, once like bulging dishes, narrowed and deepened, sinking back into the head. All four legs lengthened, muscles appeared where before was only baggy flesh. The great beast opened its mouth and roared, a blast of furnace heat that withered the distant foliage either side of the princess but left her unharmed.

Oleana-tarli quivered with excitement, her heart pumped scolding blood through her limbs, into her skull. Her skin heated like the gagrog's, she flushed pink. Her breath began to pant from her body; she felt a rising excitement, almost sexual, as her whole body throbbed. But this was better than sex, far better, her entire being stimulated, and her whole self on the edge of orgasm.

The gagrog opened his wide maw, but didn't roar, this time it seemed to stretch its jaw. And teeth appeared, not just peg teeth, but huge, man impaling canines, rising up from beside the bone. Up they stretched, clicking and cracking into place.

It stopped. Lowered its head. For a few moments all was still apart from the thundering of hearts and the hissing of rapidly drying mud. Quite suddenly, a layer of skin burst into flame along the creature's head and back. It burned away in an instant, leaving two deep channels revealed. Within could be seen four long, white, bone like appendages.

The gagrog began to stamp around, widening the circle of drying soil and burning vegetation. It roared, and Oleana-tarli felt a tingle of pain along her spine, up into her skull. Still the vision remained, the gagrog and her, charging into battle, stamping, crushing, burning everything that stood in her way. And she astride the beast, protected by the fabulous horns.

With one last roar and a stamp that shook the whole island, they appeared, rising from the back and top of the beast's skull, four beautiful horns, emerging from their hiding place of the last who knew how many years.

Oleana-tarli walked forwards, unsteady legs treading the hot ground. She saw nothing but the gagrog, felt nothing but comforting warmth. With one hand outstretched, she placed her palm against the face of the gagrog. Its skin was searing, she wondered how a creature could be so hot yet still live. But she herself, on checking her hand, was unhurt. The princess smiled widely. Her heart merely racing now, she stepped past the head and walked along the side, running her hand along the much-changed hide. It was tight now, burned free of clinging parasites and loose skin, shaped over muscles the size of she herself. All around she walked, pacing out the length of him, as she was surprised to discover, in no uncertain terms, as she walked behind him.

Ten of her strides long was he, from shoulder to tail. Easily four wide and an extra four paces for the head. She was impressed. Looking up she guessed him twice as tall as her royal self, not including the horns, and perhaps another of her legs on top of that.

Without thought or command, the gagrog lowered himself to the ground, leaning slightly over to allow the princess to climb on. When she was seated, the mighty beast stood, filling her heart with pure bliss. She rubbed his head tenderly, "Come on my mighty, let's go and play before we go to battle.

She was sure now, of all the things the gagrog could do, of how she would find and reach the battle site. All things were possible, for the two of them, locked mind and heart together. Nothing could stop them, nobody could stand before them, after all, who was there to match the awesome power of the mighty hadagrogida?

Twenty One

Around dawn, the misty town of Ya-Okovo was just beginning to wake. From the marsh, a large shape appeared, to those who were paying attention, which wasn't many. The shape came slowly on, but pushed before it a large bow wave, as though an immense form was hidden beneath the water line.

The gagrog, in full battle splendour, steaming the water around it, moved with a grace surprising for an animal of its bulk. Around the walkway, fishermen and hunters stretched and yawned as they prepared for another day.

A certain boat, flat bottomed and high in the water, showed no signs of life, but if anyone listened closely they would have heard a gentle snoring coming from a hammock strung across the deck.

With not a hand span of deviation, the bow wave headed straight for the boat like a giant arrow, cutting through marsh growth, submerging floating plants and scattering every creature able to move.

Then the wave stopped.

Looking across the swamp, the hunters saw nothing, only the marsh plants reclaiming their territory.

All was quiet, apart from the odd mumbled greeting and a few coughs. And of course the gentle snoring.

The flat-bottomed boat creaked slightly, not enough to draw attention, nor to wake the occupant. A low bubbling noise from beneath the hull caused a nearby fisherman to stop what he was doing and look over. He gestured to an older man, and together they leaned over, listening to the strange sound.

A smell, like burning wood, began to drift in the morning breeze, as the bubbling grew louder. The younger man suddenly pointed, noticing the flat-bottomed boat was very slowly taking on water. They called out to any occupants, and the people around, that the boat was sinking.

The sleeper, helped along by a residue of cheap wine, continued to snore, mouth open, limbs spread wide like a dead quatropus. The haze of alcohol began to burn away, leaving a multitude of brightly coloured images. Patches of colour focused into dreams. It was hot, very hot, and a noise like thousands of people shouting buzzed in his head. A voice, suddenly clearer than the rest, shouted, "run, run for your life!" He leapt up, and launched himself forwards. Marshwater Chada found himself unable to run, looking down he saw the reason; somehow his legs had changed and now his knees bent forwards, like some monstrous wading bird. He screamed, then screamed again as something hard pushed him up and out of the hammock.

Hitting the deck woke him, or rather, landing in water where the deck usually was. Frantically he rubbed his eyes, looked around at the water, rubbed them again. He glared at the crowd who had gathered to watch, "get out of my dream!" he yelled. They laughed. Some of the folk had tied his lines as the boat sank, leaving it hanging from the walkway. But now, instead of helping, they seemed to be moving slowly backwards.

Chada looked back to where he had been sleeping. The image of a large horn thrusting up through the material of the hammock and the warm, in fact hot, water registered together. He screamed again, a loud ear-piercing lung full of fright. With as much energy as he could summon, which was quite a lot despite his state, he ploughed across the deck and scrambled up onto the walkway, using one of the mooring lines for assistance.

Glancing over his shoulder, his eyes widened at the sight of a gagrog rising up through his boat, the water boiling, the dry timbers catching fire. Just before he vowed never to look back again, just as he swore on his long deceased mother's life he would never drink again, just as his legs began to run like the wind all on their own, his brain registered the face of a woman rising majestically along with the beast. Not a woman, the woman, the one he had left in the swamp, the one he had helped find Hadagrogida, the one who was now riding the legendary beast. And she didn't look like she had come to pay him his bonus. Marshwater Chada ran like he had never run before, pounding the wooden planks like a drum down a cliff.

The early risers stared in amazement as fire ignited out of the water, engulfing Chada's boat and spreading up the ropes. Luckily, the lines snapped before the damp walkway could catch, causing the boat to sink slowly, hissing and fizzing as it went. It finally settled on the bottom, just the peaked cabin roof showing, still burning a bright yellow flame, giving off a pleasant fruity scent as the appleoak wood was consumed.

All was still; the large shape and the big horns had gone. All eyes turned now to the retreating back of Chada, the famous marsh guide, known for his ability to survive anywhere.

Chada ran on, sweat pouring and soaking through his clothes. It ran in his eyes, stinging, blurring his vision. But still he ran, convinced he was running for his life. Don't look back, he chanted to himself, don't look back, just get away from the water. With his blood pounding in his ears, his heart rising in his chest, Chada dragged up the last of his energy and surged off the walkway onto dry land. His momentum carried him another hundred or so paces before his complaining body finally gave in. His legs buckled and he collapsed into a heap, rasping deep breaths through dry passageways. For a few seconds, he lay still, looking up at the sky and waiting for his heart to stop beating one continuous pulse.

The ground under his palms shook. His heart skipped a beat then leaped into his throat. Oh no, he thought, not land as well. The rumble grew louder, his whole body bouncing as it neared. With a greater will than he thought he possessed, he struggled to all fours, and began to crawl away, thoughts of aiming for rocky ground flitting around his mind. At the moment, the only rocky ground he could remember seeing was the mountains some three days travel away. His mind divided, one half carried on crawling towards the peaks, the other screamed no, it's too far! No, we are going to die.

Soil and pebbles rained down on him, as the gagrog emerged, bursting through the soil as though it was water. See, his mind screamed again, we are going to die. You might be, replied the other half, but I'm going to the mountains.

Slowly, heat rising, the grass withering and burning, Oleana-tarli watched Chada whimpering and crawling away. She laughed; men were so pathetic when you got down to it, only good for one thing, and not much good at that. How she wished she could take the gagrog to bed, feel it's massive prod burning as it pushed into...no, keep your mind on the job girl, pleasure later when you are queen.

Out of his mind now, Chada's body moved him forwards by instinct as the beast drew nearer and nearer, the heat burning the flesh from his feet and legs. He cried like a child as the towns folk stood, mouths agape, watching this monster from the swamp pursue the famous guide. Some produced weapons, but without effective leadership they milled helplessly around.

Finally, a shout of triumph and pleasure ringing around the still air, the monster dashed forwards, trampling Chada into the ground, front legs first, then the back. Oleana-tarli reversed the gagrog over the spot again, for good measure, then turned to face the town. Those few with weapons quickly hid them as she scanned the crowd. "No one here brave enough to stand against a woman?" she demanded. No one spoke.

The princess sat atop her living throne for a good long while, as though studying the town, wondering whether to flatten it like she had Chada. She had already decided she had more important things to do, and wouldn't waste any more energy on this hole, but let them quake awhile longer.

Eventually, she turned the gagrog and walked it slowly along the bank, then back into the marsh, sending up a cloud of steam as hadagrogida entered the water. Now, she thought, now I know the secrets of the gagrog, now we travel to war, to bring death unto the emperor and his puny armies.

A large crowd soon gathered around the remains of Marshwater Chada. His body was so deeply trampled and so badly crushed it was almost impossible to separate him from the ground. In the end, the people of Ya-Okovo simply dug up the block of soil that contained him and moved it to a suitable location. A statue was carved, paid for by the local merchants, of a gagrog being killed by a man with a long spear, and placed over the grave. Chada became legend, much like the gagrog, and the travellers flocked in.

Part Three

Magic At War

One

On the plains to the west of Esh, a large army had gathered. Surprising to the captain of the emperor's forces because they were men from the kingdom of Iamunaya.

No one on this side of the border had expected such a large force could have been brought across the land called Death; indeed no one had really taken the king's threats seriously. So it was that captain Saratil found himself the senior officer for miles around, and worse, found himself to be very short of men.

Still, he was comforted, an empire soldier was five times the fighter of a Iamunaya soldier. A nagging voice, mostly kept at the back of his mind, asked the question 'what if they have six times as many men?'

The initial battle had gone well, with many of the king's own being captured or killed. From somewhere though, those men had found others, and the army he now faced was most definitely up to strength.

They were arranged on the plain in a long line, three or four deep, a row of spearmen in the front row, a line of archers behind. From his vantage point on a low hill a few hundred paces from Esh, the captain could keep an eye on his own men, arranged in blocks, crossbow men to the front in three rows, lying, kneeling and standing, supported by spearmen and soldiers with more traditional sword and axe.

He was going to be surrounded, there was no helping that, but this way at least he could spread out the enemy lines, and do more damage quickly. The three rows of crossbow men had proved very effective in practice, each row reloading in turn whilst the others continued shooting. Let's hope it proves so in a real battle, he thought. He had no doubt the blocks would stand, keep formation until the last man went down, they were good men.

He also had a small force of cavalry, half of which stood ready before him, the rest inside Esh, waiting his command should they be needed. Hopefully, the enemy were unaware of the existence of those inside, but it paid never to assume anything in war.

And, of course, the one thing he had that no army of the kingdom would ever have, was wizards. Quite a group of them, some in the squares, some forming a loose cluster just before the cavalry. Many of them had been in Esh or the surrounding country, some had just turned up. What magic they used to get here he didn't ask, he was just glad they were on his side.

If he stood up in his stirrups, captain Saratil could just see the taller of the two women wizards who had arrived earlier to warn him about the invasion. So far they had proved invaluable, getting the town gates closed when all looked lost. They were certainly talented for their age. He hoped they would both be fine after the battle. Not just for his own sake, they were pretty, especially the shorter one, but they were also brave and deserved to live a full life.

A shout went up from the king's lines. Suddenly hundreds of men were on the move, shouting, cursing, stamping the ground as they approached. The captain's men stood firm, silently watching the advancing enemy. Let them wear themselves out; by the time they arrive they'll be breathless.

Behind the advancing army, many hundred archers bent their bows and shot long arrows high into the air. Each shaft was tipped with a bodkin head, smeared with a thick black substance. This sticky mixture was part pitch, part sap from a semi-desert plant. The pointed heads drove down onto the emperor's ranks, punching through armour, shield, and flesh, cracking, piercing, burning and bubbling the tissue as the sap spread around the wound.

The emperor's archers returned the favour, dropping heavy-headed arrows onto the approaching enemy. But none of these shafts were poison tipped; the emperor would never have allowed such a dishonourable weapon to be used by his own. Instead, these arrows were barbed; a row of small, backward pointing teeth lined each edge. When pulled from the flesh, they did more damage than when they went in. The poisoned arrows soon stopped coming, either the archers had ran out or they were too wounded to pull a bow. Either way, this left the emperor's men to target the foot soldiers.

Screams rang out from the front row as wooden tipped metal pierced flesh.

But still they came on, a look of hatred in their eyes, for now they were close enough to see, to hear the individual curses.

Now came the signal for the crossbow men to fire. The light, hand spanned weapons proved more than their worth. The king's men visibly slowed as the three-row barrage ate into the lines.

When each man had only four bolts left, the shooting stopped, the crossbow men pulled back between the spearmen, and the battle was joined, hand to hand.

K'treema and Shemaz watched intently as the squares of men were quickly surrounded by the enemy. This is all in the plan, they both told themselves, all as it should be.

Now it was their turn. They had been told to move in behind the enemy as they attacked the squares, to come up from the rear and take the enemy by surprise. K'treema was a little uneasy about attacking from behind, until Shemaz reminded her that the men they would be attacking were armoured and carried large weapons. K'treema quickly saw reason and was one of the first to reach their targets.

The noise was thunderous, as shouts and screams mingled with the sound of clashing weapons. Death threats and death cries hung on the still air. Metal splintered wood, flesh, and bone. Metal screeched on metal.

K'treema gathered her power. She had decided to try and narrow her attack, to make it more effective over a wider area. So instead of a fist, she pictured a quarterstaff, whistling through the air, landing with a dull thud on broad backs. Before her stood a forest of armour clad men, pushing and jostling for a place at the front. Their feet churned up the once fertile grass into sods and scores. Briefly she thought how stupid it was, fighting your own men to get to the front and be killed. But that's men for you she added.

As the rest of the wizards caught up and formed a loose triangle behind her she released her power, sending a vague shape slamming along a row of at least two-dozen men.

The one's to her left, where she had started, crumpled sideways, as though cut down by a massive blade, though thankfully there was no blood. Further along the effect diminished until the soldiers at the end merely fell over and lay on the ground looking up in surprise.

Shemaz stepped in next, along with an elderly woman who looked too old to be out never mind in battle. But her manner was confident, and soon the now turning rear ranks were rushing around screaming and batting their heads as though attacked by a swarm of wasps.

Beside the old woman, Shemaz whipped up a tiny storm, slamming it into the ranks and sending men flying in all directions. To the sides, the soldiers had realised they were being attacked, and were coming towards them, anger burning in their eyes. "Death to witches!" they yelled, and ran in to attack.

The wizards to the sides wasted no time in throwing up walls of fire, lines of glowing ropes and jagged lightning bolts. The attack faltered, those men still alive stood shaking their weapons and calling vile threats.

With a small shiver of disgust, K'treema tapped the magic in the necklace, drawing on an infinitely larger reserve of power than she usually had available. She stopped herself thinking about the imagined consequences and kept her mind on the battle. The front of the line of wizards widened as the others, eager for battle, strode forwards. K'treema formed the quarterstaff again, letting energy flow into her from all around. A steady shape appeared before her, an almost solid image of a length of seasoned wood. With a gasp, she released the pent up energy and slammed the image into the enemy line. Several dozen soldiers were knocked backwards, many not rising again. She kept that thought firmly separated from her conscious mind.

Shemaz was also drawing the power Dhomag had given her, feeding it into a spinning whirlwind, not bothering to wait for the ribbons to arrive, but grabbing them with her increased ability, and throwing them into the rotating wind. A soldier, braver or more stupid than the rest, broke free of the line of cursing men and dashed towards the wizards. His sword swung in an arc towards the old woman, caught unawares as she concentrated on her magic.

Before he could finish the blow, he was lifted from his feet and spun back to his comrades, sword still gripped in his outstretched arm. Many of his countrymen died on the whirling blade as it scythed through their ranks, until the man had the sense to let go, or was killed, as armour and weapons and loose arrows flew all around. And still Shemaz drove the wind, as she never had before, she felt the power surge, not just from the necklace, but through it, drawing on the power available to the mage. Not as much as him, not the black and life blighting force that Dhomag drew on, she couldn't match his power anyway. So she convinced herself, she was doing more good than harm, saving the country from being over run with barbarians, preserving the peace. A few years of blighted crops was fair payment for that surely?

Then suddenly before them stood the emperor's men, grim faces breaking into grim smiles as their eyes fell upon the wizards. Shemaz pulled back her whirlwind just in time, directing it to one side to take in a few of the straggling enemy fighters.

K'treema and Shemaz stood with arms linked, leaning

against each other. They were both bone tired, but still felt a small pull of magic from their necklaces. They didn't have the strength to summon more power, although Shemaz's now small whirlwind was still spinning a few paces away. The soldiers had drawn back from the wizards, preferring to throw themselves onto metal than face the magic.

"I think we've done our bit, can we rest yet? I'm so tired I could sleep in a puddle."

Shemaz nodded, "me too, but we better not leave until the rest do. Anyway, the soldiers may come back, we need to be here in case they do."

K'treema nodded, closing her eyes, trying to block out the noise of people dying.

Two

And the battle raged. Metal to metal, to leather, to flesh and bone. Magic energies blasted into metal and flesh, melting and melding. The king's men were out matched by a superior force; supported by wizards, by better training and discipline. Many times the lines would have broken if not for the sheer number of the Iamunayans.

Still the emperor's forces prevailed, slowly but surely biting into the king's own, reducing their numbers at a much greater rate than their own losses.

Underfoot, the ground rumbled, a ripple of thunder fallen from the sky. So focused were the soldiers that the first roar went unnoticed, as did the second. But the third was stronger, causing the wizards to stop and look down at the ground. The fourth and fifth were even stronger, sending a crack along the floor amongst the feet of the fighting men. Now they noticed, now they turned to see, as a great fountain of earth was forced high into the sky behind the Iamunayan front line.

Those closest tried to run, but were knocked from their feet by the earthquake that thundered around the widening hole.

Movement was seen; something huge began to rise up from the earth. Soldiers scrambled in all directions, even towards the enemy just to be out of the way as the ground heaved and shuddered. A great heat began to spread from the hole, the moist soil steamed and dried, the organic matter burned.

A gigantic head broke the surface, horns like sharpened tree trunks, eyes afire, a mouth that breathed a furnace breath. The ground ignited as the gagrog burst from the soil, planting its mighty feet on solid ground.

The soldiers backed away, leaving a wide area around the beast. Strangely, a woman sat between the horns of the beast like a queen on parade, her long legs bare, her hair blowing in a non-existent wind, her whole face lit with wild triumph.

A line of crossbow men was revealed as the king's soldiers scattered. With the greatest of discipline, the men fired their quarrels in strict order, the first row re-loading whilst the second fired, they in turn re-loading as the third row discharged their bolts. Many hundred bolts were aimed true towards the gagrog, and the woman, but none reached their target, burning up instead in the intense heat.

The king's soldiers had realised that the gagrog was somehow on their side, and began to fall in behind it, to follow it into battle. The emperor's pike men formed a line, five rows of long pole arms, each set for charge against the ground, pointing towards the beast. Quickly now, building up speed, the gagrog came on, setting fires as it thumped down its massive feet.

The pole arms skidded along the hide of the beast, or had their heads torn off where they snagged. Not stopping or even slowing, into the pike men it stormed. The cracking of bones joined the cracking of wood. Blood boiled in the heat; handfuls of soldiers were impaled as the gagrog shook its giant head. Its mouth opened, those not snatched into its maw were burned alive by its searing breath. And still it ran on, lumbering towards the command position, ignoring the soldiers that ran along side braving the heat, stabbing or shooting into its impenetrable flanks.

The wizards rushed forwards, casting spell upon spell into the fiery behemoth, all to no avail. The magic energy seemed to be repulsed by the crocodile like skin of the creature. The woman was seen to smile as the monster thudded on unstoppable, burning a wide swathe as it progressed. The wizards turned their attention to her, but the spells were repelled by the mere presence of the gargantuan beast. On came the gagrog, not a thing done by the men even slowed it, not a weapon or spell could touch it, the woman riding on its head laughed, a wild, cheering sound. The king's men laughed too, driving into the emperors disarrayed forces with glee.

A roll of thunder sounded, a great cheer arose from the king's army, who looked expectantly downwards for another of the creatures. But this thunder came from the sky, from a black cloud approaching from the east. A bolt of white lightning burst from the cloud, illuminating the entire battlefield. Thunder sounded again rolling across the ground, buffeting the men with sound. The cloud dropped from the sky, like a rock down a cliff. It landed on the ground with an audible thump.

Another strike of lightning, this one lasting longer than anyone had remembered lightning lasting before, lighting the area brighter than a summer noon. The light finally went out, leaving behind darkness as dark as the light had been bright. Thunder boomed and boomed again, ground shaking, ear vibrating, roll after roll until all present stopped what they were doing to cover their ears. Light flashed inside the darkness, a single, almost too quick to see pulse of searing white. Moments later another flash, then another, faster and faster until the cloud of darkness disappeared.

Blackness came again as the light suddenly stopped. Complete silence fell across the field, even the gagrog had stopped, the woman on his back leaned forward from her position, a deep frown on her face.

From out of the darkness stepped a man. Tall, broad shouldered and handsome. A massive sword strapped across his back was the only weapon he carried, he wore no armour, no boots or gloves. Confidently, he strode towards the gagrog.

The woman astride the mammoth beast looked towards the man and scowled. She seemed to recognise his power, if not his face. With a single gesture she turned the beast towards the newcomer, spurring him on with guttural cries.

The gagrog ran faster, its legs blurring with speed, pounding fire into the ground as it moved.

The man walked to meet it, he too began to run, eyes locked on the creatures, arms and legs pumping faster and faster.

The woman yelled a shrill battle cry, calling her army to victory. The soldiers responded, breaking off the fighting with the emperor's forces, a fire in their bellies calling them on to greater glory.

They neared, the gagrog hammering the ground with feet of flame, the man skimming the grass with barely a sound. The woman screaming now. The man silent and expressionless. Great horns and teeth and a blazing maw hurtling towards a man who, as yet, hadn't even drawn his sword.

Closer, ever closer they came. Those watching stood dumbstruck; those charging fell behind, the fire all used up.

A few more paces and they would meet.

A sudden flash of metal was seen and the man had the sword in his hands, it appeared as though it had leapt straight from scabbard to grip in the blink of an eye.

The length of the blade, held high before him, turned white with a glittering frost, shedding a fine powder of snow into the light breeze.

The man felt the heat of breath against his cheek and

the gagrog was upon him.

Down came the blade, slamming into the gagrog's face as it opened its mouth to bite this pretender.

The sword buried itself up to the hilt with a deafening hiss, clouds of vapour poured out, burning away on the gagrog's hide. The beast bellowed with rage and pain. Not missing a step, its charge continued, pushing the man backwards, raising clouds of dust and clods of earth around his feet.

The man twisted the sword, sending more steam hissing into the air. The woman screamed, as if mortally wounded. She rose up, standing against the horns, her face pained and drawn.

Still the gagrog ran, thundering and roaring at the man, trying to bite, to trample, to impale. But the sword was buried deep, and the man's grip was tireless. Still on his feet, sliding as if on ice, the man rode the brute, twisting the great blade, each turn a fresh hiss of ice on fire, each turn more ice and less heat.

The woman slumped, almost toppling onto one of the mighty teeth. The gagrog slowed, the fire damping with every step.

Finally it stopped, the fire extinguished.

The man stepped back, examined his handy work, and withdrew the sword. Ice glittered along its length. Dhomag looked at the blade and smiled. Sheathing the sword, he approached the beast and gripped one of the teeth. With a loud crack, Dhomag ripped the tooth from its roots, slung it over his shoulder and walked away.

Oleana-tarli lay slumped on the dead beast, her insides numb with cold. A tear ran down her cheek and froze; a word mumbled from her lips, softly, just once, "Father."

* * * * *

Dhomag strode towards the still approaching army, and realised they were still approaching. Their weapons drawn, they seemed to be rushing straight at him, shouting for revenge. Several hundred men, all angry, incensed and senseless.

Dhomag found himself annoyed more than anything; he was just about to claim his glory, fortune, and a night or two of pumping with two very attractive wizards.

He threw down the tooth, drew his sword and relaxed, feeling the flow of power. His body became a conduit to the massive river of energy within the planet. The first of the soldiers neared, and was cut down by a wide stroke of the sword, yet the man had been no closer than thirty paces.

Dhomag swung the great blade again. What a worthy sword he thought, a mighty weapon for a mighty warrior. The power flowed faster and faster as more soldiers ran at him, trying to over bear him with strength of numbers.

The magic poured through the conduit, surging through the mage with a feeling like pure bliss. Dhomag was enraptured; he never wanted the feeling to end. He could have turned every soldier on the field to boiling liquid with one gesture, but chose instead to wield the sword, channelling the magic through a smaller area to allow him longer to enjoy the feeling.

On they came, by the dozen and by the score, by the hundreds, and still they were cut down. Bones and body parts gathered all around him, although he wasn't aware of turning around. In wider and wider arcs the sword swung, as though the blade was lengthening. Each swing cut through ten, thirty, fifty men as the power roared through the mage. Men began to slip and trip on the gore, and suddenly the attack had stopped, the men finally seeing sense scrambled to get away. He cut at them as they ran, singling out individual soldiers and cleaving them in two, down the middle and from side to side, or quartering them with a rapid double stroke.

Dhomag looked around, at the piles of body parts, at the surprisingly small amount of steaming blood, at the fleeing soldiers. He leaned the sword against his shoulder and walked towards the centre of the battlefield, avoiding the gore by floating above it.

The few of the king's soldiers who had survived were in disarray, dropping their weapons and fleeing, or surrendering to the emperor's men.

Words came to Dhomag's memory, from deep within, etched into his soul.

I vow to kill the emperor.

And the magic burned.

Dhomag turned towards the line of the emperor's forces, towards the few men stood on higher ground. He didn't know if the emperor was present, didn't care, it was a good place to start.

A blue sheen raced along the blade of the sword, ice crystals crackled and flaked. The next minute the ice was burned away by an intense blue flame. Dhomag walked on, his face an image of concentration. The ground blackened or froze as he strode on, leaving a strange trail behind him. His face was alight with power, his eyes sparkling with rainbow flecks of light.

"Dhomag."

A voice disturbed him but he ignored it.

"Dhomag! What's wrong?" Someone tugged at his sleeve.

The sword leapt into the air, crackling with ice and flame in quick succession, he locked on the target and swung the blade, bringing it crashing down on the figure beside him, the figure who had dared to interrupt him.

A split second before the blade struck his eyes fell on the figure's face, the image registered on his mind a split second later.

K'treema.

The blade began to bite into K'treema's sleeve just below the shoulder, into the skin.

Dhomag released a thump of energy along his arms, the blade of the sword shattered into dust. The hilt in Dhomag's hands continued around, travelling the path the blade would have taken.

He looked into K'treema's face. Her eyes were filled with tears of pain, she had gone quite white. Shemaz was standing slightly behind her and to one side. Her mouth hung open and she constantly switched her wide eyes between Dhomag and the small trickle of blood on K'treema's arm.

For the first time in a thousand years, Dhomag felt pity, sorrow, and another's pain.

"K'treema, I'm sorry, I wasn't thinking. Here, let me look." Dhomag peeled apart the edges of her sleeve and began to examine the neatly sliced cut on her arm. It wasn't deep, but was bleeding nevertheless. Shiny flecks of metal glittered as the red blood seeped down towards her elbow, the dust of the shattered weapon.

Shemaz stepped forwards, finally able to move. "Can you heal it?" She asked abruptly.

"I don't think so, the power doesn't seem to appear when I think of healing. I can burn it shut if you like?" Dhomag raised a finger, the tip glowed sunset red and fizzed with energy.

"No!" the wizards shouted together.

"I'm fine, it just needs binding, it's not deep." K'treema continued, pulling her sleeve over it and clamping on her hand protectively.

"It will need cleaning, who knows what this mage got on the blade." Shemaz complained.

The three faced each other, eyes flicking from one to the other. No one spoke for a while, until Dhomag's puppy-eyed expression made K'treema laugh "Its all fine, Dhomag, really, just don't do it again. And leave the emperor alone, we told you he was a good man."

Dhomag looked relieved, his expression returning to its normal, unfathomable neutrality.

"What now?" K'treema asked.

"Well, I vote we carry on with our Journey, we are still a long way from home, there's a lot to learn yet," Shemaz suggested.

"I think we've seen enough, but I don't suppose

anything more exciting will happen between here and there. What about you Dhomag, which way are you heading?"

"I think I'll go back to the desert. I've got a lot to think about, and that seems the only place where the memories come back. But I will see you again, I'll come and find you when I'm more settled, when I know more about who I am. And tell the emperor not to worry, I realise now it wasn't the same one, nor any relation." He smiled, the warmest one he could manage. "I don't suppose you would consider going to find a quiet spot somewhere and the three of us having a few hours of naked passion?"

K'treema and Shemaz looked at each other, back at Dhomag, then at each other again. "Yes, come on then. I hear some of those taverns in town can be very comfortable, and I don't suppose any one will be bothering you for a while," Shemaz giggled.

"And as long as you keep your magic to yourself. And, I can't believe the way you got here, talk about making an entrance. Couldn't you have just walked?" K'treema asked. Dhomag merely smiled, then the three of them linked arms and wandered off towards Esh, watched by hundreds of pairs of bewildered eyes.

* * * * *

In a hole some distance from the battleground, Falco Tarm cowered in a dark hole. I really must stop doing this, he thought to himself. A long shape moved in the shadows, pulling itself from a narrow slit in the side of the hollow. With so much speed Falco was unable to react, the shape plunged long fangs into his bare hand, sending rushes of hot agony tearing up his arm.

A single word drifted into the silence above, as deep convulsions shuddered through Falco's body.

"Arse!"

Also by this author

From Hadesgate Publications

Soulkeepers

The Servicing and
Maintenance of Wayland
Snowball

From ForeverpeopleRPG

Faerytales – An anthology of short stories
Wilderness Encounters 2 – In the Mountains
Wilderness Encounters 3 – In the Desert
Contributing Editor to Wyvern magazine
Co-writer of 'Heroes of Trollstone' with David Sharrock